we GO
LIQUID

we go LIQUID

CHRISTIAN TeBORDO

IM•PE•TUS
press

Impetus Press
PO Box 10025
Iowa City, IA 52240
www.impetuspress.com
info@impetuspress.com

978-0-9776693-3-2

cover photograph, design and
text layout by Willy Blackmore

September 2007

Sometimes, late at night, when the rest of the neighborhood has been cussed to sleep and the counting sheep are silent, when summer rain drips to the roof and trickles toward the gutter, when the house is so quiet that I can hear electricity trying to force its way into novelty appliances I haven't touched in years, Jane Grundy emerges from radio static to taunt me.

"Are you awake?" she says. "Me too. Your father again. He's got a message for you:

"'Sing through your toes, son. Tell them our story. Bleed it onto paper like I bled out on the couch while you ran around the neighborhood trying to avenge me.'"

He's mocking my hope, but some nights the very thing we would mock becomes the object of our nostalgia, and as the lights flicker with the surge of the stainless steel coffee-maker in the kitchen, we mistake mistakes for lessons and death for a change of phase.

So I've removed my socks with my teeth and placed the keyboard on the floor, in case his death and my survival were not in vain.

THE
MINIATURE
HUSBAND

The first email I received from my mother after her death
was on the impersonal side. In fact, I'd received it, or one
a lot like it, before, from an African gentleman with whom
I'd struck up a long-distance friendship. At least I'd thought
we were friends, though it had started out with a business
proposition.

He said he was a high-ranking Nigerian diplomat
hoping to immigrate to the United States, that during the
course of his career, he had accumulated fifty million dollars,
all by legal means, but that the other Nigerians would be
angry with him for taking the money out of their country. He
said that fifty million dollars was a lot of money, and that if I
would allow him to deposit it in my checking account until he
managed to get to America, he would be happy to let me keep
ten percent of it.

Of course, I knew that fifty million dollars was a lot of
money, and I knew that it was probably more than the average
Nigerian diplomat, even a high-ranking one like Amos—that
was his name—could earn legally in a lifetime. But I also

knew that five million dollars was a lot of money, practically
as much, to someone whose total income, between allowance
and mowing lawns, was twenty-five dollars a week at most, as
fifty million.

The problem was I didn't have a checking account. I
had a junior savings account at the Hudson Valley Savings
and Loan. My father made me deposit anything over ten
dollars that I made each week at the end of every month.
It was growing slowly because the ten dollar cap was a
disincentive to getting all sweaty and sunburned mowing
Mrs. Malatendi's lawn when she hardly ever went outside
anyway. I think I had about two hundred dollars in there at
the time, and I was sure that someone would notice if there
were suddenly fifty million two hundred dollars in a junior
savings account.

My parents, on the other hand, did have a checking
account. But I wasn't about to bring the subject up with them.
By their rules, there wasn't even supposed to be a subject. By
their rules, I wasn't even supposed to open, let alone answer,
an email from a stranger.

So I answered it:

> Dear Mr. Amos,
>
> I am sorry but I am twelve years old
> and do not have a checking account. If you
> ask your other friends and they do not have
> a checking account either, you can email me
> again and I will ask my parents who have a

checking account. I hope that you make it
to America because it is a good place.

I didn't hear back from him about the checking
account business, and so after a while—I don't know how
long—I forgot about him.

Until I received a second email, which led me to
believe that his venture had been successful, and he had
arrived safely in the United States. I don't remember what
it said exactly. Because of my father's rules, I deleted
every email I received from a stranger, every email that I
received, even though I didn't consider Amos a stranger
after that first email.

The subject header read: "Let's go to the movies."

The same subject header as the first email I received
from my mother after her death. The content of that email,
which I saved, because my mother was not a stranger,
at least I didn't consider her one, despite her death, and
because my father had by then pretty much forgotten I
existed, read, in its entirety: "Free movie tickets!"

As I said, I don't remember exactly what Amos' said,
but it had the same message, if not the same wording.

So I answered it:

Dear Amos,
    I am glad that you have made it
to America and get to see free movies.
Unfortunately I will not be able to go to

the movies with you for free because my
parents will not let me go to the movies
with strangers. Or email them. But we can
still email each other.

That was the last email that I ever received from
Amos, and I forgot about him again until I received
the same message from my mother. Even then I didn't
remember him right away. I had something more important
to think about. It was my mother, and she was dead.

If it hadn't been past my bedtime I would have
screamed for my father. As it was, it was past his bedtime
too. He'd started going to bed, actually the couch
downstairs, early after the death and the funeral. It had
only been a month, but it was already a pattern. My
sleeplessness had become a pattern too. I was staying up
later and later, looking for something. And when I found it,
I didn't know what to do.

I sat there for a long time, just staring at the screen,
so long that my vision started to blur and I almost nodded
off. I wasn't tired. I was overwhelmed. I wanted to hit the
reply button and tell her that I missed her, that I thought
my father missed her, but I didn't really know because he
didn't talk to me anymore, that I hoped that she could get
three free tickets so we could all go together. I wanted to
ask her where, when, what did she want to see, and could
we maybe get some pizza afterwards and talk? Could she
come home with us, or did she have to go back? And if she
had to go back, where?

I hit the reply button.

I typed: "Mom."

I didn't want to make her as overwhelmed as she'd made me. If free movie tickets was enough to get me that worked up, then my barrage of questions might scare her away. Or make her feel guilty for begging them all. I didn't want her to feel guilty.

I deleted: "Mom."

I typed: "Mom?"

I sat staring at the screen again, longer than the first time, as more and more questions presented themselves. Would I recognize her? Would she be a person or a ghost? Could she even go? After all, it just said "Free movie tickets!" On the other hand, the subject header said "Let's," as in us, as in me and you, or me and you and your dad. Was this someone's idea of a fucking joke?

"Mom?"

I pressed send. I pressed save. I signed out, logged off, put the computer to sleep and went to bed.

I lay there for a long time before falling asleep, as long as usual, trying to count sheep, but every one of them came with a new question. Still the possibility that one of them had an answer was better than what they usually had to say.

My mother had always had trouble sleeping, too. I didn't know whether she still had trouble sleeping, but when I awoke at 4 a.m., it seemed plausible that she might have been doing the same thing I'd been doing when I got her email, that she'd already replied.

I sat up in bed. I thought about it again, about how it would feel if she hadn't replied yet, whether I would be disappointed, whether I could keep myself from feeling like she was never going to.

I slipped out of bed. I slipped out of my room and walked slowly down the hall toward the computer, trying to be as quiet as I could, though I didn't imagine my father would hear me either way. I thought I heard something in the living room. I say I thought, because I couldn't describe now what I thought I heard.

I stopped short and listened. The sound of my own breathing.

But as I listened to my breath, a silhouette emerged from the shadows of the living room, a body in profile, standing at the end of the hallway facing the kitchen doorway, until it turned and faced me.

My father. I knew it was my father, but I didn't know if he could see me. There was no light in the hallway—no windows. What light there was was coming from behind him, the palest moonlight, maybe a streetlamp.

There was nothing to be scared of. I was scared. I stepped backwards, feeling along the wall for the door of my room until I got there, got in, closed it behind me as quietly as I could, and hid beneath the blanket until the sunlight came through my window and turned it yellow.

I didn't leave my room until I heard my father leave for the pharmacy. The door slammed, the car started and

sped off; I ran to the bathroom and peed like I'd been
holding it in for hours because I had. That taken care of,
I walked down the hall toward the computer, sure that my
mother had had a chance to email by then, but when I got
there, I just stood in front of it, occasionally fingering the
keys, but hesitant to wake it up.

I remembered suddenly that I was supposed to mow
Mrs. Malatendi's lawn, ran back to my room, dressed, and
left the house. Outside it was warm, but not unbearably so.
It was the beginning of my summer vacation and mornings
were still cool enough for lawn mowing to be relatively
comfortable, but I had to pull the throttle three times to
get the mower to start, and I cursed under my breath as
the motor puttered to life, afraid that Mrs. Malatendi might
have seen me through her window and decided to make
one of her rare trips out of doors to make sure I didn't spit
on her grass, and to point out where I'd missed a spot.

Throughout the mowing season, I alternated between
making ever-narrowing concentric rings around her yard,
like a racetrack but more wobbly, and latitudinal rows,
which were neater but less interesting. That time, I was
doing rings on the front lawn, almost enjoying the way
that they spiraled in on each other until I had to pivot the
mower on its back wheels three times to get the last little
patch.

The sun was higher in the sky, and I was getting
sweaty and frustrated. As I jerked the mower around a
corner, tearing up a clump of sod, I started thinking about

how long it would take my mother to reply.

I was sure it was only a question of how often she got to use the computer, if they had scheduled times like I did at school, or if they had regular access in their own rooms, or if she had to sneak in, and then delete everything she got, like I did.

I went on like this until it finally occurred to me to wonder who "they" were, and I had to acknowledge to myself that I had been imagining that the dead had email access. From there I began to wonder whether all of the emails I got were coming from the dead, whether Amos had not made it to America after all, but had somehow died in his attempt to smuggle his fifty million dollars out of Nigeria.

Before I knew it, I had shut off the mower, leaving the back yard half done, and was running across the street into my house, tracking grass shavings up the stairs and jumping into the chair in front of the computer. I woke it up, telling myself that it didn't matter if my mother hadn't replied yet, that she would get back to me as soon as she could, that I needed to apologize to Amos, in case I had mistaken his death for a move to America.

I typed:

> Dear Mr. Amos,
>   Last night I received an email from my mother who is dead. Are you dead?
> If yes, I am sorry I mistook you for an

American and please tell my mother I
miss her.

My mother hadn't replied.

I reminded myself that that wasn't the point. I clicked refresh. Still no reply. I thought about emailing her again. I clicked refresh. Nothing.

The doorbell rang.

I looked over my shoulder, as though I could see from the living room who was at the front door. All I could see from the living room was the rest of the living room, the hallway to the bedrooms and bathroom, and between the living room and hallway, the door to the kitchen on one side and the staircase leading to the landing, which was also the entryway, on the other.

I looked back at the computer. Another knock and the door opened.

A voice said, "Hello?" like a foot testing water.

It was the voice of a girl, a bored sounding, monotonous in just two syllables, put-upon voice. Maria Malatendi, sent, I was sure, to complain about my unsound lawn-mowing methods. Maria was Mrs. Malatendi's granddaughter. They lived alone together, without Maria's mother or father.

Rumor around my locker had it that her father was a military man. Had been a military man until he told when he wasn't asked. I didn't know what that meant, but it sounded significant, significant enough to convince

me that the rumored results—his discharge, his murder
of Maria's mother, his attempt at murdering Maria by
strangulation with a camouflaged boa before the SWAT
team stormed the windows of their faraway home, his
arrest, his conviction and committal to an institution for
crazy old soldiers—were true.

She was older by a grade, headed to high school in
the fall. I didn't think much of her, and I doubt she thought
much of me, because one time one of the other guys at
the bus stop had dared me to ask her if the rumors were
true. They never talked to me unless it was to dare me to
do something stupid, but every time they did, I thought it
might be the one that would earn their respect.

I tried to be as delicate as possible, but she just
flipped me off.

That wasn't the worst I'd gotten at the bus stop.

"Hello?" she said.

I didn't respond. I hoped that she would hear me not
respond, not hear me at all, decide no one was around,
and report back to her grandmother, assuming that I'd had
good reason to take a break from my work—a drink from
the spigot or the faint tinkle of an ice cream truck in the
distance.

Instead she made her way up the stairs instinctively,
or because every house in the neighborhood was laid out
on the same plan. I turned around as I heard her steps,
and our eyes met as hers rose up over the floor of the
living room. I could see them between the thin black bars

of the railing.

"Hello?" she said again, and again I didn't respond.

She reached the top of the stairs and stood staring at me. We stared at each other. She broke away first when a chill ran over her, and she looked around as though confirming something that she'd expected.

"It's cold in here," she said.

She went into the kitchen, and I went back to the computer. I clicked refresh. Nothing. I heard her rummaging in one of the cupboards, and looked over my shoulder, but all I saw was the empty living room, the hallway. The cupboard closed. The thuck of the refrigerator opening. A pause and then liquid hitting the bottom of a glass, filling it. Something thinner than milk, but not fizzy. Iced tea or water.

"What are you doing?" I said.

Gulping, gulping, gulping. The sound of a glass being set on the counter. A satisfied but desperate exhalation. She came back into the living room and walked toward me nonchalantly. I minimized the window. She stopped behind me, looking over my shoulder.

"What are you doing?" she said.

"Nothing," I said.

She reached over me and put her hand on my hand. My hand was on the mouse, the cursor was on the window. She clicked, and up came my mother's email. We stayed like that for a moment, her hand still on mine, her breath breezing past my ears toward my nostrils: sweet, iced tea-scented.

"I thought she was dead," she said.

"She is," I said.

Maria moved our hands. Our hands moved the mouse. The cursor's arrow glided over the blank space of the email and became a hand over the text. "Free movie tickets" went from black to blue beneath it. Maria clicked.

Up popped a new window, full of bright colors and moving images. A bucket of popcorn with arms and legs and a face that took up an entire cardboard panel, twirling an unspooled roll of film like a gymnast in one hand, holding the hand of an effervescent cola with long fluttering eyelashes in the other. They were dancing toward a box office on the other side of the window, beneath a marquis that read "Free! Free! Free!"

"Spam," said Maria.

I froze. She removed her hand and stood up straight.

"My grandmother wants to know why you didn't finish the lawn," she said.

I just sat there watching the popcorn and cola. They kept dancing toward the box office, but they didn't seem to be getting any closer. Still, they looked happy. They were in love, and they had everything they needed.

"My grandmother wants you to finish the lawn," she said.

"In a minute," I said, and she left.

I didn't make it back to the lawn that afternoon. I sat there for a long time watching the happy couple, hoping they'd finally make it to the movies, but they never did, and when I decided that they never would, I closed the window, hit refresh a few times—still nothing—put the computer to sleep and laid on the couch thinking about I-don't-remember-what.

My father got home late, dusk, almost dark. Mrs. Malatendi must have been waiting for him by the window the whole time because she was across the street and walking up our driveway before my father even got out of the car.

I looked out the window when I heard the door slam, and saw them talking—my father slumping, looking tired with his back to me, Mrs. Malatendi gesticulating with one hand and supporting herself on her cane with the other. The conversation seemed one-sided. I couldn't hear a word my father said—maybe because he was facing away from me, maybe because he was speaking quietly—but occasionally I heard Mrs. Malatendi's voice, indecipherable but old-woman-whiny.

It didn't last long. Within a couple of minutes they were parting ways, my father turning and heading up the walk toward the front door, still slumped, his shirt wrinkled, the top button undone beneath his tie, his labcoat rumpled over his arm, and Mrs. Malatendi turning and hobbling across the road with a couple of glances back. She might have seen me watching from the window, but I don't think so—the lights were off in the living room and the sun was all the way down, and I assumed that her sight was no good in the first place because she was always handing me one dollar bills for the tens she owed me despite her supposed skill in spotting unmown patches of grass.

My father walked into the house, up the stairs, and into the kitchen without a glance my way. I heard him rummaging in the cupboard like Maria had, and then he poured himself a glass of milk. I knew it was milk because I watched him from the doorway. I watched him take a sip.

"What was that about?" I said.

My father choked, and milk dribbled down his chin. He looked my way and said, "I didn't see you there."

"Sorry," I said. "What was that about?"

He took a sip of his milk. I watched him closely, as though there might be an answer in the action.

"What?" he said.

"In the driveway. With Mrs. Malatendi," I said.

"She wants you to mow her lawn," he said. "Today."

"It's dark out," I said.

"That's what I told her," he said.

The next morning, I checked my email before I mowed the lawn. Nothing from Amos. Nothing from my mother. Either someone was cracking down wherever they were, or Maria was right and it was spam.

I thought about it as I finished up Mrs. Malatendi's back yard. At least, I thought about it whenever I was out of sight of her kitchen window. When I was in front of the kitchen window all I could think about was how creepy it was the way she stared at me, like maybe she was as crazy as her son. Maybe crazier. Maybe it was diluted from one generation to the next. Then again, maybe it only got worse.

I decided to lock the doors from then on to make sure Maria couldn't just walk in whenever she felt like it. I decided there was so much craziness in her family that she could easily be wrong about everything, especially my mother's email. I wondered if I'd gotten any emails while outside.

I got so distracted wondering about emails that I forgot to knock on her door and collect when I was finished. I put the mower back in the shed, and ran into the house. I forgot to lock the door too.

I'd only been watching the popcorn and the cola

proving Zeno's paradox for a couple of minutes when Maria walked in without even knocking. She said, "Hello," as she walked up the stairs, but I didn't look up. She went into the kitchen, poured herself a glass of iced tea, and came out into the living room, sipping lady-like this time. I was still watching the computer.

"If I hadn't seen you mowing the lawn I'd have thought you were doing that the whole time," she said.

I didn't respond.

"My grandmother says you missed a patch of grass near the maple tree," she said.

She'd succeeded in distracting me. My thoughts were no longer with the junk food lovers, but my eyes stayed there, pretending, convincingly it seemed. Maria got more interested. She thrust three fives between me and the computer screen and said, "I should keep some of this for having to bring it all the way over."

I snatched the bills from her hand and placed them carelessly on the desk, but I left the mouse unattended as I did it, and Maria reached it and clicked it shut before I even noticed what she was doing. I felt her chest against my shoulder blade. She had breasts.

"Are you gonna go?" she said.

"Where," I said.

She sighed deeply, dramatically. Iced tea breath again.

"To the movies?" she said.

"Why?" I said.

"Didn't your mother invite you?" she said.

"She's dead," I said.

Maria slapped the back of my head.

"You're the one who said it was spam," I said.

"You're the one who said it was spam," she said, in a baby-talk voice.

Did I sound like that? Did I sound like that to her?

"It says free," she said.

She clicked the link again and pointed at the screen, at the marquis that said "Free! Free! Free!" As she reached over, she pressed into me more firmly. Her lips tickled the down of my ear. I don't think she had any idea of what she was doing to me.

"Do you want to go or not?"

Was that an invitation? I imagined us walking hand in hand toward the "Free! Free! Free!" marquis and never getting there, never getting tired of the feel of her hand in mine, never getting tired of the way her long eyelashes fluttered when I looked into her eyes.

But she didn't really have long eyelashes, and this was about my mother. I tried to play it cool.

"How would I get there?"

"We could walk," she said.

"We?" I said.

I couldn't press it any harder.

"It only takes forty-five minutes to get to the mall," she said, misunderstanding or ignoring my question.

"When?" I said.

"Tomorrow afternoon," she said. "I'll be over after lunch."

We made it to the marquis, halfway, then halfway again, and so on until we were there without a brush of the hand or the flutter of an eyelash. I think it was me who avoided eye contact like it would kill me. Maria walked beside me with the same bored nonchalance with which she had walked into my house uninvited and poured herself a drink two days earlier, which she'd done again that afternoon before we left.

I was at the computer as usual. The popcorn and soda hadn't gotten any further, but I was watching with intent this time. It had crossed my mind that I had no way of proving that the tickets should be free. My mother still hadn't replied.

Maria took a sip of her iced tea and said, "Still looking at that thing?"

"How will they know we're supposed to get in free?" I said.

Maria leaned over and put her hand on the mouse. There was no contact because my arms had been crossed as I'd sat there trying to find the answer, the code. Her chest didn't press into my shoulder blade. Either she was avoiding me, or the previous days' touching had been an accident. The whole thing started to seem hopeless. My stomach was empty, and I felt nauseous.

She waved the cursor over the scenario but nothing changed. No new links, no secret password, no revelation. She gave up. Her hand slipped back to her side. She stood up straight.

"We'll just tell them," she said.

I tried to hit refresh without her noticing. Nothing.

"Let's go," she said, and we went.

Needless to say, the marquis did not say "Free! Free! Free!" It said a lot of other things, twelve in fact, twelve movie titles, one for each theater, some of them repetitions. Maria and I stood looking up at them, far enough away to take them all in at once.

It was cool inside the mall, too cool in contrast to the weather outside, which was just warm enough to make you sweat if you walked a mile and a half. The sweat was drying at my temples, crusting my hair there, and when my shirt brushed against my back it stuck and gave me chills.

"It should be something about death," said Maria.

She said it matter-of-factly, as though it was an obvious part of our plan, a plan that we had already discussed, as though merely restating something that had been decided well before we'd left my house.

"Why?" I said.

"Your mother's dead," she said without looking away from the marquis.

I didn't want to respond to that, but I was about to when Maria pointed upward. I followed her finger to the title and read.

"They won't let us in," I said.

"Why not?" she said.

"It's rated R," I said.

"PG-13," she said.

I pointed to the sign she was still pointing to and watched her eyes slide right to the place where the rating was.

"R," I said.

"The sign's wrong," she said, grabbing my arm and jerking me toward the ticket counter. We walked to the sign that said LINE FORMS HERE and went through the maze of fake velvet ropes instead of going straight to the only open window, even though the place was empty. I guess it seemed more adult.

The guy behind the window couldn't have been much older than Maria. His hair was stringy, and he had one of those puberty mustaches that looks like dirt smeared on your upper lip.

Maria said, "Me and my little brother won two free tickets for *The Sixth Sense*."

"IDs," said the guy in the window.

"For PG-13?" said Maria.

The guy pointed to the sign behind him which again showed that at least someone at the theater thought the movie was rated R. Maria shook her head, more disappointed than angry, but started to pat her thighs as though feeling for something in her pockets even though she was wearing a long skirt and didn't have any. I didn't bother pretending. I was fuming about the little brother thing.

"Shit," she said. "I must have left it at home."

"No ID, no ticket," said the guy.

Maria summoned her most grownup expression, the kind you use when you tell a waiter that what he brought isn't what you ordered.

"But they're free," said Maria, "we won them." It didn't make any sense, but the guy in the window was flustered. He just stood there until Maria broke the silence.

"I want to talk to your manager," she said.

The guy seemed almost relieved. He said, "Just a second," before disappearing through a door in the back of the booth.

I was wondering what Maria was planning to do when the manager came back, but Maria wasn't planning on being there when the manager came back. She grabbed my arm again and jerked me toward the lobby.

The only person behind the concession counter was a girl about the same age as the guy from the ticket booth. Maria pulled me through the lobby and let go once we were in the dimly-lit hallway that half of the theaters branched off of: in the clear.

The one we were looking for was all the way at the end, on the left. I kept looking over my shoulder, nervous, but Maria told me to stop because it just made us look more suspicious. Still, my heart didn't slow down until we were seated in the shadows in the back row of the empty theater, and even then I didn't feel entirely comfortable. I had to go to the bathroom but couldn't risk going back out toward the lobby, especially not without Maria.

We hadn't checked what time the movie was supposed to start. The previews hadn't begun yet, and the theater was silent except for the thin, inorganic music piped in to let the audience know how loud to talk. Maria talked louder, but still in a monotone.

"See," she said. "Free free free."

"I don't think that's what it meant," I said.

But then something happened that made me think that was exactly what it meant.

"Anyway," said Maria, "it was free."

I wasn't paying attention to her. My eyes were on the tall, dark man who had just entered the theater through the door to the front. He was wearing an usher's uniform—black pants, a white shirt, and a red vest—and carrying a flashlight, which was redundant because the houselights were still up.

But none of that concerned me.

What concerned me was the way he walked, like a marionette made to look like a skeleton, and his eyes. They stared bright and sad from the blackness of his face. I had seen that walk, those eyes, before, in the television commercials that ask you to adopt a child from a third world country, and I knew that the usher was from a Third World country in Africa, and I knew that the usher was Amos, and I didn't know what to do, but I stiffened.

Maria sensed it, the way my elbow jammed itself into

hers on the armrest. I had never initiated contact before. I hadn't meant to then. She left her arm where it was, against mine, even though it must have hurt.

She said, "What?" and I didn't answer, so she looked up at me, and then she looked where I was looking.

She said, "Shit."

For some reason I assumed she was saying it for the same reason I was thinking it, that she knew as well as I did that the usher was either an embezzling diplomat from Nigeria whom I'd refused to abet as he emigrated, or that he was dead, that this movie theater employed ghosts, that my mother could be in the ladies' room, handing out paper towels for tips.

"Look around for a ticket stub," said Maria.

She dropped to the floor and started to scan it with her hands as Amos started to scan the theater with his eyes. They passed me twice, like spotlights in a movie, before landing on me alone, in appearance if not in truth. Amos pointed his flashlight at me and flicked it on. The beam was dim by the time it reached me and I didn't even have to squint. Still, it made me uncomfortable, and I squirmed as though preparing for an interrogation. He spoke with a thick accent.

"Are you here with a parent or legal guardian?" he said.

"It's PG-13," Maria hissed, quiet enough that he couldn't hear.

I thought of my mother in the bathroom, waiting,

towel extended, for some woman to finish washing her
hands.

"She's in the bathroom," I said.

Maria patted my shoe.

"Good," she whispered.

"I'll be back to check," he said.

He switched the flashlight off, let his arm fall to his
side, and gangled slowly out of the theater.

"Is he gone?" said Maria.

"Yeah," I said.

She was up in a flash, standing over me, looking
down.

"You fucked up," she said. "We have to go."

I was about to remind her that she'd encouraged my
cover only a minute before, when I realized that I didn't
really want to convince her otherwise. I wanted to go too. I
stood up and followed her out of the theater.

When we stepped into the hallway I saw the rectangular
lightbox indicating the women's room at the other end.
As we got nearer the doorway it hovered above, I couldn't
shake the idea that my mother was in there from my head.
I knew it was just my imagination, that I had made it all
up as a cover, but there wasn't a doubt in my head that the
usher was Amos, and I'd had no reason to believe he'd be
there either, until he walked in.

"Don't you have to go to the bathroom?" I said.

Maria gave me a look like disgust, to let me know
that she was still mad at me for ruining her free movie
scheme, and that I wasn't helping anything.

"It's a long walk home," I said.

She ran ahead without even acknowledging me. I
thought she was going to leave me to walk home alone,
but she veered right at the lightbox and stormed in. She
must have actually had to go but was too proud to admit it,
because she took a long time in there.

I got kind of awkward standing outside the door like a
miniature husband. I tried to look adult, like I hadn't just
run out of a movie because of an usher I thought was dead.
As I waited, I remembered that I had to go too. It hit me
suddenly, an unsubtle reminder like a fire in my bladder,

but I reminded myself that this wasn't about urination, it was about my mother.

By the time Maria came out I was bent half over with one leg crossed in front of the other. Still, my first thought was about whether she'd seen my mother. I tried to sound casual.

"Anything interesting in there?" I said.

She gave me the disgust look again.

"Let's go," she said.

I tried to stand up.

"I have to go too," I said.

"I'm going," she said.

I watched her walk into the lobby and assumed she'd leave the mall and head home alone. I turned to go into the men's room, which was directly across the hall, but stopped. I turned back to the women's room, looked both ways, and jumped in.

It was empty. No one using it—I peeked under the doors. No attendant. No mother. I went all the way to the stall furthest from the door and sat on the warm plastic seat, imagining that it was my mother who had warmed it, though it was probably Maria, if the seats weren't naturally warm. I finished and washed my hands and wished my mother was there to hand me a towel.

Maria was in the hallway, facing the men's room, when I exited. It should have made me feel good but it didn't.

"Hey," I said.

She turned and saw me standing in the doorway.

"Gross," she said.

I tried to repurchase her affections by getting us dinner from McDonald's with my lawn mowing money, and she accepted the food, but the walk home was even less romantic than the walk there.

I didn't expect Maria back after that, and when our usual
time arrived the next day and passed without a knock at
the door, or the door's opening without a knock, it seemed
like a confirmation. I had been sitting at the computer
pretending to look at the email from my mother, the first
one, but by then I'd pretty much given up on that too.

I don't remember how I killed the rest of the
afternoon, but I remember thinking, when my father got
home from the pharmacy, that I hadn't done anything all
day.

"What'd you do today?" said my father.

But I only thought about it, didn't tell him. Because
he wasn't really asking.

"What's for dinner?" I said.

"I'll order a pizza," he said.

By the time the delivery man got there, my father
was asleep on the couch downstairs. I didn't know it yet,
so I answered the door. Maria was standing behind the
pizza guy, a plain pinewood box dangling from her hand
by a thin plastic handle. She walked around him, past me,
into the house and up the stairs. I heard the thuck of the
refrigerator door, a cupboard open and shut.

I was surprised, but hungry, and I had to take care of

business before figuring out what she wanted.

I called out: "Dad!"

He didn't answer.

I went downstairs and found him asleep, his face buried in the plush arm of the sofa, the afghan my grandmother had knitted us tangled around his legs.

"Dad," I said.

I shoved him, tried to rouse him, but he didn't wake up. I went back upstairs to see if maybe he'd left the money in the kitchen. Maria was still there, waiting for me. There were two glasses of iced tea on the counter beside her, but no cash.

"Do you have any money?" I said.

"What for?" she said.

"Pizza guy," I said.

"Ask your dad," she said.

I explained to her that I'd tried to, but that he was asleep and wouldn't wake up. She guided me back downstairs, past the puzzled pizza guy and over to my father.

She went up to him and shoved him herself, whispering something, I don't remember what, just that he roused without waking up, and before shoving his face back into the sofa, he said my mother's name.

Maria jumped back and said, "Sorry."

I don't know to whom.

She ran up the stairs. I heard muffled voices, then the door closed. I figured Maria had left, and wondered what she'd said to get rid of the delivery guy. When I finally decided to go up to the kitchen to see what I could scrounge together for dinner, she was standing on the landing with the pizza box in her hands.

We ate in silence, but it wasn't awkward. The pizza had cooled and the iced tea had warmed, but I was hungry. I hadn't eaten all day.

When we were finished, Maria cleared our places while I wrapped the leftovers in foil and put them in the refrigerator. It was starting to get dark out by then.

Maria said, "I guess I should get going."

I didn't want her to, so I stalled, trying to think of a way to keep her there.

"Do you want me to try to wake my dad up again?"

It was the wrong thing to say. She cringed then tried to cover for it.

"Why?" she said.

"To pay you back," I said.

"Tomorrow," she said, and then she left.

It made me happy to think that I would see her again the next day, that I had a reason, an excuse to. I hadn't been thinking about romance. Even when she'd touched me, I'd thought of my reaction as a reaction to her touch.

But it was becoming a full-blown crush, which made me nervous. I'd had plenty of crushes before, but none of them had ever made a habit of dropping by my house or acknowledging me. And she was older, more experienced, I assumed.

I started to get overwhelmed, almost to the point that I hoped she wouldn't get over the creepiness of my sleeping father, so I checked my email to try to distract myself.

Nothing. Refresh. Nothing.

I clicked and clicked again until the sun finished setting and the room darkened, until there was nothing left but the blue-white glow of the monitor, and I was drowsy enough that I thought I could sleep.

Of course, I forgot to get the money from my father the
next morning. He was off to the pharmacy before I woke
up, and then I was running around the house, searching
counters and cushions for cash or spare change. As I
bolted into the kitchen, still empty-handed, I tripped over
something and went flying to the floor. I looked back to see
what it was before I was even back on my feet.

The pine box that Maria had brought over the day
before.

I picked it up and set it on the counter by the door,
running my hand along its unfinished edges as though it
might help me guess what was inside. I lifted again and
shook it a little. It rattled, but nothing telltale.

I wasn't going to open it. I told myself I wasn't going
to open it. It was Maria's, Maria's business. My hand
reached for the copper latch, my thumb rubbed against the
smooth, tarnished button, but couldn't bring itself to apply
any pressure. I couldn't bring myself to either. I rushed to
the computer, consoling myself with the idea that at least I
would have something to give her.

Click. Nothing.

Back in the kitchen—no click. Nothing.

The computer. I clicked reply.

I typed: "Mom."
I deleted it.
I typed:

Mom?

I don't know if it was really you who
sent the email. The one that said free
movie tickets? We tried to go, but they
were not actually free. We got in anyway,
but then Amos was there and he is dead
like you.

Do you know Amos? And also, do
you work in a bathroom?

I forgot to tell you that we is me and
my girlfriend Maria. Not really but I hope.
Do you think I should look in her box
without her permission? She is a little bit
older.

I hit send, stood up, and went outside for the first
time in two days.

It was warmer than it had been, hot even. I sat on the stoop and tried to pretend like I was happy sitting on the stoop, but really I was trying to see in the windows across the street, knowing I was risking making eye contact with Mrs. Malatendi but hoping to see Maria. All I saw was the glare from the early afternoon sun. It was the time of day that Maria had come over those first couple times.

The stoop was hot beneath my ass. Two of the guys from the bus stop, Joel Danes and Barry Russell, coasted by on their bicycles. I started to wave. I don't know why. I'd never been on friendly terms with either of them. Neither acknowledged me. I looked down at the ground to save face. There were red ants on the ground. I stood up, brushing myself off, but I didn't want to go inside.

I could see from where I was that Mrs. Malatendi's lawn didn't need mowing, but then thought it might look shaggier closer up. I walked across the street. It didn't need mowing. I looked up and caught Mrs. Malatendi glaring at me from an upstairs window. I looked away fast, and walked back to my house, trying to seem nonchalant.

I had to go in then.

The box was still closed. No reply from my mother. The box was still closed.

Maria didn't come by that day. My father came home, but I didn't have to order any pizza—there were leftovers from the night before. He was asleep by the time I was done eating, and I was left alone to wait. She didn't come that night either. I gave up around eleven.

As I lay in bed trying to fall asleep, I wondered why she hadn't come over when she'd said she would. The only thing I could think was that my father had freaked her out more than I'd thought. I decided he was going to have to do some making up for it.

I went downstairs and stood over the couch, over his body on the couch. The news was on, something about how great everything was—the economy, the government, the people, everyone was happy. I reached to the floor beside the couch, picked up the remote, and turned off the television.

I said, "Dad."

No response. I shook him.

"Dad," I said.

When he didn't wake, I pulled the afghan from his legs. He was lying on his stomach, fully clothed. My hand gravitated toward his pants, his back pocket. It was gross, but I had to do it. I stuck my hand in and came out with the wallet, stuck my fingers into the wallet and came out with a twenty. I couldn't bring myself to put my hand back in his pants, so I left the wallet on the floor beside the remote.

I put the twenty on the kitchen counter beside Maria's box and went to bed.

Back in bed it wasn't any easier falling asleep. I tossed and turned. I tried counting sheep, but the sheep wouldn't behave the way I told them to. They kept saying box instead of baaa.

I said, "Say baaa, sheep," but they wouldn't.

They wanted me to look in the box. It got to where it was almost painful. I'd stopped counting after three hundred, but they kept coming, each one wailing: "box." And they didn't stop once they'd jumped. They just joined the rest of the herd, screaming without cadence, no voice melding with another and none distinct from the group, so that it became impossible to make out what they were saying, but I knew, because I'd heard it so many times already, because I wanted them to say it, because I wanted to know what was in there too.

I made my way down the hall with the feel of my hands against the wall and flipped the light switch in the kitchen. I stood over the box, hesitant, squaring its edges against the edges of the counter, then pushing it back an inch, keeping it parallel, but framing its pale pine against the darker faux-wood finish it was resting on. I put the thumb of each hand against each button and pressed. The latched flipped upward.

"What are you doing up so late?" said my father.

It wasn't accusatory or angry. In fact, there was barely a trace of a question in his sleepy question, but it startled me and I stepped backward. The box stayed closed.

"I couldn't sleep," I said.

He nodded.

"Me neither," he said.

But of course, he could. It was just about all he could do as far as I could tell.

"What's in the box?" he said.

I don't know why I pretended I knew. I guess because I felt guilty, because I was guilty, of invading Maria's privacy. Even if she'd meant me to look, I was looking without permission. I tried to come up with an answer that sounded true, while being vague enough to seem true if he made me open it.

"Just some stuff," I said.

He reached for the lid, not like he didn't believe me. He didn't even seem curious. It was more like a half-assed attempt to show some interest in me. He opened it.

From where I was, I couldn't see into the box, so I didn't know what was in there.

"I didn't know you were into art," he said.

Neither did I.

"Yeah," I said.

He gave me a sad smile and let the lid close gently.

"Try to get some sleep," he said.

"You too," I said.

His back was already turned, and he raised a hand to me as he made his way down the stairs, taking a step, bringing the other leg to meet it, taking another step, like he was as crippled as he was exhausted.

I took a step forward and lifted the lid. It was full of art supplies—paper, pencils, pastels, crayons, some other things that I didn't recognize—stuff. I let the lid close, lowered the latches, and went back to bed.

I didn't wake up until noon the next day. No email from my mother. I showered, dressed, shoved the cash in my pocket and grabbed the box by its skinny plastic handle. I left the house and went across the street to Mrs. Malatendi's.

It was warmer than ever, as warm as summer gets, I think, the sun barely past directly overhead. I was sweating just standing in front of the door. I was nervous, but before I had the chance to press the doorbell button, the handle slipped from my moist palm and the box fell to the stoop, popping open, its neatly stowed contents spilling to the ground.

I squatted down and started shoving things back inside. I was still down there when the front door opened. I looked up through the glare of the still-closed storm door to see Mrs. Malatendi staring down at me.

She said something through the plexiglass but I couldn't make it out. I used one arm to sweep the rest of the art supplies into the box and crammed it shut.

"Pardon me?" I said, standing up.

She still didn't open the door, but I heard her more clearly this time.

She said, "It doesn't need mowing yet."

"I was wondering if Maria was here," I said.

"What?" she said.

I opened the door.

"Can I speak to Maria?" I said.

"Maria's not here," she said.

I stood there dumb, wondering where she could have gone. I didn't know what to say next.

"I'll tell her you stopped by," said Mrs. Malatendi.

She closed the front door, leaving me standing there with the box in my hand, still propping open the storm door. I finally let it close and went back across the street, sweat-drenched.

I'd meant to sit on the couch by the window and watch the
street until Maria came back, for signs of where she might
have been, but the air conditioner was so cold and my skin
so damp that I started to shiver pretty violently. I grabbed
the afghan from the back and as I warmed up I fell asleep.
I awoke to the sound of my father's car door slamming. A
glance across the street and there was no sign of whether
Maria had returned or not.

I heard the front door open and my father's feet on
the landing.

"I ordered Chinese," he said.

I heard his feet on the stairs, headed down.

I must have nodded off again, because the next thing
I heard was the doorbell's ring. I woke up groggy, but with
enough presence of mind to expect the delivery guy. The
sun was only just dipping behind the Malatendi house.

I went into the kitchen to grab the cash I owed Maria
from the counter. It wasn't until I saw it wasn't there that
I remembered having shoved it in my pocket earlier. I
walked down to the landing, opened the door, and paid.

I took the food upstairs without even bothering to
try to wake my father, though from the weight of the bag it
was clear he'd ordered more than enough for the both of

us. As I took a plate from the cupboard and scooped some rice and some oily chicken from the paper containers, I wondered when and if my father was eating. He didn't seem to be thinning, but then you tend not to notice weight loss in someone you see every day, even if you barely see him.

I dropped my fork on the plate and went downstairs.

He didn't look any thinner, sprawled, asleep, on the couch. I crept toward him. His right arm was hanging over the edge, his hand resting on the floor. I stared at his wrist. I reached out and touched it. I tried to wrap my fingers around it. The thumb and middle finger just missed meeting.

I tried the same thing with my wrist. The middle finger pressed into the pad of my thumb. My wrist wasn't as big as his. But it didn't seem like a very big difference.

"Dad," I said.

He didn't answer.

"You need to eat, Dad," I said.

He didn't wake up, but I hoped that at least his mind would absorb the message, like when my mother used to read my study sheets to me as I slept the night before a big test.

I can't say for sure it worked, but I did pretty well in school, and my father walked into the kitchen as I was finishing up my chicken.

"Food's here," he said.

"You wouldn't wake up," I said.

He pulled a plate from the cupboard and brought it over to the table. He sat down and placed the plate in front of him.

"How'd you pay for it?" he said.

I figured he hadn't noticed the twenty that went missing from his wallet the night before.

"Lawn mowing money," I said.

He reached into his back pocket and pulled out his wallet as the front door opened. He didn't seem to notice and went on rifling through the bills. Maybe my hearing was more sensitive to Maria, seeing as how I'd spent the previous three days listening for her.

"How much?" he said.

I wasn't paying attention as he pulled the twenty out and passed it toward me because Maria had come into the kitchen. She saw it dangling in the air above the table and snatched it from my father's fingers. That's when he noticed her.

He seemed uncomfortable, but not surprised.

"Hi, Melissa," he said.

Neither of us bothered to correct him. Maria shoved the money into the pocket of her jeans as my father stood up and kind of bowed before heading to the stairs.

"Don't stay up too late," he said without turning.

"Your dinner," I said.

He said, "I had a big lunch," and kept descending.

Maria sat down in his chair and started scooping food onto his plate. When she had a good-sized portion she stood up and looked around. For a second I thought she was going to bring it to my father, but instead she said, "Fork."

I pointed to the drawer. She grabbed one and set to. After a few bites she said, "Eat."

I showed her my plate. She watched the sticky residue slide across its surface and a drop hit the Formica, then went back to hers. I got up, took two glasses from the cupboard, and poured iced tea, setting one in front of her. She didn't notice or ignored it until her plate was empty. Then she swallowed it in two gulps and clacked the glass on the table like a cowboy in a movie.

I took the glass and went over to the refrigerator.

"You're probably wondering where I've been," she said.

My hand trembled as I poured and some iced tea splashed to the floor. I placed the glass on the counter beside the sink and grabbed a paper towel, stalling, hoping she'd explain herself without my taking the bait as I wiped the floor.

No such luck. I tried to play it cool.

"I've been pretty busy," I said.

Maria frowned. I placed the glass in front of her.

"No thanks," she said.

She went over to her box and opened it, looking through as though to make sure everything was there. I knew it was a mess, because I hadn't tried to reorganize it after spilling its contents in front of her grandmother and then shoving everything back in, but I tried to pretend like it wasn't me.

"What's in the box?" I said.

"A mess," she said. "Like you didn't know."

I wasn't even going to try to contradict that.

"No," I said. "I mean what's it for."

She lifted it by its handle and carried it into the living room saying: "Come on."

So we scribbled. Actually, I scribbled, she drew. I looked over at her sketchpad every now and then and saw a reasonable approximation of our living room coming into perspective. I don't know why, but it made me admire her. I was starting to go from wanting to be her boyfriend to feeling like her little brother, like it wouldn't be so bad to be her little brother.

She looked up and caught me staring. I realized I'd been transfixed awhile and snapped out of it.

"I have to build a portfolio for art school," she said.

She was going into ninth grade in the fall.

Suddenly the whole scene seemed impossibly quaint, like playing with Legos or reading the encyclopedia to get smarter or singing at recess. I wanted to watch her border the drawing with Elmer's glue, to feel her breath on my skin as she blew gold glitter from the page, to listen as she cut through construction paper with safety scissors.

"It's good," I said.

"Don't patronize me," she said without looking up.

I didn't know what patronize meant, but in context it seemed like a way of saying things, so I said nothing, took out another sheet and scribbled some more.

It was dark by then, but I didn't realize how late

it was until I finished a drawing of a skeleton on white construction paper with a black crayon—the one I always did when they told us to draw in art class—and looked up at the clock. It was almost midnight.

"It's almost midnight," I said.

Maria looked up at me, then over at the clock as though she had to see for herself to believe it, then down at my paper. I immediately regretted saying it. I didn't want her to leave and I was sure she would once she realized the time.

"I'm used to staying up late," she said.

It seemed like she was fishing for a specific reply, like a sincere *you're really grown up*, but I couldn't figure out a way to say that, or anything like it, sincerely, so I sat there in silence, and tried to show her that I was interested.

"When I visit my dad," she said. "That's where I was the last two days."

She must have caught me catching on that one. I was still under the impression that her father was criminally insane. But instead of going on when she saw me recompose myself and wait for an explanation, she stared me down, as though challenging me to confront her with my truth. So I did:

"But your dad's in prison," I said.

"No," said Maria. "He's on a mission."

"He killed your mother," I said.

Maria said, "He's coming back this summer and

we're going to find a new house."

"He tried to kill you," I said.

"So I probably won't see you again after that," she said, "after we move."

I didn't know what to say. She sounded delusional, like the family insanity hadn't skipped a generation. I probably would have just sat there in front of the sketchpad forever, my shoulders slumped, my mouth hanging open, if she hadn't spoken up.

"The guy from the movie theater," she said.

I looked down at my paper. It did look something like Amos — his shade, his posture.

Maria stood up and stretched. I started to pack up her box for her.

"What are you doing?" she said.

"Don't you have to go?" I said.

"I'm just turning on the radio," she said.

She went over to the stereo, flipped on the power, and started to spin the knob toward the left end of the dial. She stopped on the Jane Grundy Show.

It was a call-in program I'd barely heard before my mother died, mostly around the edges. My mother or father, sometimes both, would tuck me into bed, and later in the night, sometimes an hour, sometimes more, when I'd get up to go to the bathroom or get a glass of water, I'd hear Jane Grundy's voice without knowing whose voice I was hearing, and sometimes I'd hear laughter from my mother or father, sometimes both.

Once, not long before my mother died, having heard
them laughing so hard I almost started laughing too,
standing there in the moonlit hallway with an empty Dixie
cup in my hand, I snuck into my bedroom, turned the
radio on, but quietly, and wound the dial until I heard that
distinctive voice.

Jane Grundy had a voice like a cartoon character,
or the host of a children's television program, somebody
with a name like Cranberry Muffins or Henrietta Von
Waterracket. But she didn't talk like a cartoon character.
Her vocabulary was so profane that I have to remind
myself she was broadcasting out of our neighborhood, that
she was little more than a glorified ham radio operator, to
keep from wondering why she wasn't fined or locked away.

The caller was female. She sounded nervous, like
she was looking over her shoulder to make sure no one was
watching, even if she was home alone. I only caught the
end of her complaint. Something about the cat's claws and
the furniture or the carpet.

I don't remember Jane Grundy's answer either, but I
do remember some of the words she used. I'd heard fuck,
thought I knew what it meant, but I'd never heard it on the
radio, never heard it uttered by a voice like Jane Grundy's.
I giggled to myself and it made me feel grown up. Asshole
I knew too, but I could feel the grin spreading on my face,
and I might have slapped my knee.

I lost it the second she said cocksucker. I had no
idea what a cocksucker was, but it sounded bad and it

sounded funny and it sounded like something I could get into trouble for saying. I burst out laughing, repeating cocksucker and laughing harder, so hard it was hard to breathe. That's how my parents found me—rocking back and forth on my back, on my bed, red-faced and breathless, but still mouthing the word: cocksucker, cocksucker. I'd been right to think I could get in trouble for saying it. For hearing it, too.

So I hadn't turned it on since, even though the rules had loosened up since my mother's death. My father probably wouldn't have noticed if I'd played it in the same room with him. Still, it seemed best not to listen to it in the living room. The laughter might wake him up.

"If you want to listen to that, we should go in my room," I said.

I said it before I'd even considered the implications, but once the thought was out in the air I was embarrassed, scandalized for the both of us. Maria shrugged, grabbed her sketchpad and headed down the hall. I turned off the stereo and followed.

Fortunately, my room was pretty neat. It always had been. Up until then I'd never done much of anything but sleep in it, and I'd gotten into the habit of making the bed in the morning once my mother wasn't around to hound me about it any longer.

Maria had already switched on the little alarm clock radio on my nightstand and was sitting on the floor starting a new sketch, this one of the stuffed lamb on my bed. The lamb was hardly recognizable as a lamb because I'd slept with it bunched in my fist every night for as long as I could remember, and I was embarrassed by its ugly, mangy appearance and also by its existence. But Maria didn't say anything. To her it just seemed like something else to draw.

The caller on the radio was a male, and he was asking if he shouldn't put all of his investments into gold, just in case. Jane Grundy let loose a flood of obscenities that didn't seem to have anything to do with the market, and I laughed. Maria just smirked and continued to draw.

We kept listening, or I did, and Maria kept sketching, and I practiced smirking instead of laughing. By the time Maria was done, I had myself pretty well under control.

Summer went on like that. Maria left her box in my room and returned to use it nightly. I started to acquire my own materials and even a little bit of technique. I liked weird juxtapositions—Maria and my stuffed lamb, for example, usually in some religious context, like the Annunciation. I didn't really know that there was a tradition of religious art. Maria told me.

We listened to Jane Grundy nightly, often until she signed off, slipping in and out of attention to her and to our art. I'd gotten used to her obscenities by then, but she still made me laugh. We'd been listening to the show long enough to know that there were several different versions of callers, but mostly there were two. There was the type that was in on it, exhibitionists and people who had cooked up stories just to egg Jane Grundy on, teenagers at slumber parties hunched around a single speaker phone, some so outlandish that even at that age I suspected they were in-house jobs.

The other type was just up late at night and needed someone to talk to. Half the time they'd end up in audible tears, sobbing and sniffling into the receiver until Jane Grundy told them: "If you can't handle it, try counting sheep," breaking the connection, leaving them alone with

a few more lines of one-sided abuse before the program
passed them by altogether.

I felt sorry for all of them.

The night that Maria finally decided to call in, I
couldn't decide which one she was.

The caller sounded like an old woman. She was
telling Jane Grundy that she was ready to die, but she was
scared.

Jane Grundy said, "What the fuck is wrong with
you?"

The old woman got flustered and missed a beat.

"Obviously you're senile," said Jane Grundy.

"I'm just old," said the old woman. "I've lived a full
life."

"Heartwarming," said Jane Grundy. "And now you're
fucking ruining it, wasting your time and becoming a
burden to your family."

"I had cancer," said the old woman. "Ten years ago."

I didn't get to hear how it ended because Maria
slammed her sketchpad to the floor. She'd been drawing
the cartoon dinosaur border of my walls in meticulous
detail. She went over and turned off my clock radio.

"I was listening to that," I said.

"You have to turn it off when you call," she said.

She picked up the phone on my desk and dialed.

"What are you gonna ask her?" I said.

She held up a finger to shush me. I waited, and tried
to ask again, but she shushed me again. We sat there in

silence until suddenly Maria said, "I'm an artist."

At first I thought she was telling me, and I was getting ready to agree with her, if a little sarcastically. Then I heard Jane Grundy's voice coming from the earpiece. She was loud and animated, but I couldn't make out what she was saying.

"Well, I wanted to ask my," she paused. "...my friend to pose nude for me."

Overtones of Jane Grundy. Still no sense of what she was saying, not that I could concentrate anyway, given what Maria had said. I froze, hoping she wasn't talking about me, hoping she was talking about me.

"For my portfolio."

Jane Grundy said something else, and Maria said, "Thank you." Then she placed the receiver back in its cradle, turned and walked out of the room.

I wanted to call after her, to ask her what she'd been talking about, but then I thought maybe Jane Grundy was still talking about whatever they'd been talking about, so I jumped onto my bed and switched on the clock radio.

Some old guy talking about how they don't make them like they used to, Jane Grundy saying how they never fucking did.

I rushed out of my room and down the hall just in time
to hear the front door close behind Maria. I knelt on the
couch beneath the window and watched her walk across
the street and into her place. She didn't look back once.

I didn't know what to do. I knew I would never get
to sleep that night if things stayed as they were. I knew
I needed someone to talk to, but my father was asleep
and I wouldn't have talked to him anyway. I hadn't talked
to anyone else but Maria since school had ended. But I
couldn't talk to Maria because I didn't know if I should
pose nude for her. No one but my parents had ever seen
me naked. I'd never seen anyone my age naked, so I didn't
have anything to compare myself to.

I thought about trying to find something about it on
the internet, but then worried about getting arrested. Then
I thought about asking my mother. Not directly, not about
my physique, but about my situation, what I was supposed
to do.

I turned on the computer. My mother still hadn't
responded. I clicked on the original email from my mother
and hit reply without even bothering to watch the "Free!
Free! Free!" show first. I wrote:

Mom?

I guess you don't get much time to use the computer wherever you are, cause I know you'll get back to me as soon as you have the chance.

Anyway, I'm writing because I have another question. It's about my girlfriend. Not really, but I'm still hoping.

You might remember her because I asked you about her box. I did end up opening it without her permission, but she didn't get mad. It was full of art supplies. Now we do art together because she is working on her portfolio and listen to Jane Grundy but please don't tell Dad.

I was wondering what you think I should do if she asks me to pose nude for her. She hasn't, but if she does.

I hit send, and when I did, I felt a sudden sense of peace, as though my mother would take care of everything, even though she still hadn't replied to either of my earlier emails. The sense of assurance was so strong that I went to bed right afterward and fell into a dreamless sleep without a sheep in sight.

UNPLANNED OBSOLESENCE

The second email I received from my mother after her death was a little more personal than the first, but it was also a little out of character. Not the subject matter. She'd always been very open about sex. She and my father had read me that book where the man and woman who loved each other very much expressed their love for each other on the grass beneath a full moon when I was in third grade.

No, it was the grammar.

The subject header read: "Drive her wild." The full text of the email read: "Grow your cock up to three inches bigger."

When I checked my email that morning, before I'd even seen who it was from, that message—Inbox 1—seemed like an answer to my prayer. So I wasn't immediately thinking about the grammar. What I was thinking was how did my mother know? How did she know that I wasn't worried about ethics or propriety? How did she know that my first fear was anatomy?

I hit reply.

I typed:

Mom,

It was so good to hear from you.
How do I grow my cock up to three inches
bigger?

It was as I typed that last sentence that I started to
wonder whether my mother had really written it. First,
the word cock. Hadn't she grounded me just a few months
before she'd died for hearing and saying cocksucker?
Then, as I typed "bigger," I realized that it was pretty
redundant with "grow." My mother was a stickler for
things like that.

I hit cancel.

I sat there staring at the screen, racking my mind for
an explanation until I remembered my mother's first email,
and the secret message of love between the popcorn and
soda pop. I waved the cursor over the text and it went from
black to blue.

I did an analogy: free movie tickets is to animated
junk food as grow your cock up to three inches bigger is
to blank. I didn't know if I wanted to know what would
fill that blank. I considered sitting there in front of the
computer, periodically clicking refresh until Maria came
in and clicked the link for me as she had before. Then I
realized that that could prove even more awkward than
clicking it myself.

So I clicked it myself.

Before and after.

Before and after.

Before and after.

I couldn't say for sure that before had actually led to after, because there were no faces, but it looked as though whatever was supposed to grow your cock up to three inches bigger worked.

The images were graphic and grotesque, almost frightening in their high resolution under less than flattering light, but for some reason, maybe because of how disgusting it all seemed, they helped to confirm my impression that my mother had sent it.

That left the mysteries of how she had known, why it was okay now to use the word cock, and why it was so badly written. To demystify the first mystery, I decided that a mother always knows. The second required a good deal more justification. I thought about cocks. I thought about cocksuckers. I thought about the relationship between cocks and cocksuckers until I realized that a cock was a perfectly natural thing, even by that name, even for someone my age.

I thought back to the night my parents had read me the sex book. My father had broken away from the huge font and the watercolor illustrations to ad lib about masturbation. I had no idea what the word meant, and my father must have been able to see it on my face because he went on to translate it many times over.

"You know," he said. "Jerking off? Beating your meat?

Choking the chicken?"

By then I understood, but he was still going. My eyes got so wide they started to tear up, and I bit my tongue to keep from giggling. I finally had to look away from his face, but when I did, I saw he was demonstrating the international pantomime for masturbation, the one they teach you the first day of school. I burst out laughing, just like I did later when Jane Grundy said cocksucker. That finally got my father to stop, but I got the message: masturbation was okay, like it was okay to have a cock, but cocksucking was off limits.

As for the final mystery, the deterioration of my mother's grammar, I couldn't think of anything to explain it just then. I decided two out of three wasn't bad and clicked order.

Before and after became Visa or Mastercard.

My mother knew I didn't have a credit card.

That was when I realized that my mother was losing it. As I thought about it, it only made sense—she'd been dead a few months by then. I knew enough about death to know that her body had been decaying all along, I just hadn't been thinking about it. I hadn't wanted to. But now that I had, I realized it only made sense that her mind would be rotting too. Which made getting the order in all the more urgent. I put the computer to sleep, praying that my father would get home and go to sleep before Maria came over that night.

It seemed to take forever, but he did get home before Maria. Unfortunately he had a large bucket of fried chicken in his hands and he actually seemed to want to eat.

"Hungry?" he said.

"Not really," I said.

"Come on," he said, stepping into the kitchen. "You've got to get some meat on those bones."

I stayed where I was, on the couch in the living room, hoping he would take the hint, but for once he didn't. Or did. It was hard to say.

He stuck his head out of the kitchen and said, "Come on," with a kind of desperation that made me feel almost sorry for him.

I sat in the kitchen and picked off the skin of a drumstick, trying not to betray the fact that for once I actually wanted him to go downstairs and go to sleep, and trying not think about beating meat or choking chickens.

My father was voracious, cleaning whole bones in a single predatory bite, licking them clean between grease-smeared fingers, all the while making small talk, mouth full between oily lips.

"So how's Miranda?" he said.

I glanced at the clock on the microwave. It said, 7:15. I felt a little nauseous.

"Is she your girlfriend?" he said.

"Maria," I said.

"Who?" he said.

"Maria," I said. "Not Miranda. Or Melissa."

"Sounds like you've been getting around," he said.

I rolled my eyes. My father suddenly froze mid-chomp. I didn't see it happen because I'd gone back to staring at my plate, but I sensed it and looked up.

"You're not," he said.

"What?" I said.

He just sat there, mouth open, a mash of chicken muscle on his tongue. It was so disgusting that I forgot what he'd asked. Then I remembered, which was even more disgusting.

"No," I said, hoping I sounded convincing but not wanting to protest too much.

His mouth closed and his teeth slowly ground the meat into swallowable particles. His Adam's apple bobbed up and down until he took a sip of his milk. I thought about the milk and the chicken grease and how they would react with each other in his stomach.

"Maybe you shouldn't be spending so much time alone with them," he said.

I looked at the clock again. My father didn't seem to want to talk anymore. He finished his meal in silence while I picked at mine. He cleared my place without asking if I was done, stuck our dishes in the sink and said, "Goodnight." I heard his footsteps descending the carpeted stairs.

7:45. Maria could show up any minute, but I had to wait and make sure my father was asleep before I could order. I rushed to the living room window and looked out. No sign of life from my front door all the way across the street to Mrs. Malatendi's. Their porch light wasn't on yet, but it was only dusk.

I sighed relief, if anyone actually does that. I had time, for now at least. I couldn't say why it seemed so urgent that I order that night, before Maria got there. It wasn't like I'd get the pill or ointment or whatever it was just by entering my father's credit card number, and even if I did, even if that was possible, it would probably take four to six weeks to grow my cock up to three inches longer. And what if it didn't grow my cock three inches longer? What if it was two? What if it was one? I breathed a sigh of despair. Sometimes you actually do that.

I woke the computer up. No reply. I opened the second email from my mother. I clicked on the text. Before and After. Before and After. Before and After. I scrolled down the page to the fine print: "Results not typical."

I needed to know how atypical they were and how long the results took to result before Maria got there. It was a matter of confidence, in case she walked in and said,

"Will you pose nude for me...friend?" I could answer: "I'm fairly busy working on a crucifixion of a stuffed lamb just now, but I could pencil you in for something in, say, four to six weeks." Then I would pretend that the crucifixion I'd been sketching the night before was just a study for something bigger, larger, something important, and spend the next month or so working on it, fucking up if it got too close to good or done, and as my cock expanded in my pants, my art and my sense of myself as an artist would expand until I had produced two masterpieces, one for myself and one for Maria.

The house was so quiet I heard my father snore from where he was. I glanced out the window. Nothing had changed. My father snored again, a stuttering, adenoidal sound, like the air he was trying to breathe was actually some thick, viscous liquid.

I hit reply.

I typed:

Mom,

Thank you for the offer of a thing that grows your cock up to three inches bigger. How atypical are the results? If you can find a way to make my results atypical too, I promise that I will only pose nude. No cocksucking whatsoever, even the word.

Except I do listen to Jane Grundy.

Don't tell Dad.

My father snored again. I hit send. I put the computer
to sleep. I snuck downstairs.

He was sprawled on the sofa, the afghan tangled
around his legs. But he was on his back this time, hence
the snoring. I had to figure out a way to get the wallet out of
his back pocket.

"Dad?" I said, testing the air.

He didn't stir.

"Dad?" I shoved his shoulder.

No response. I left the hand on his shoulder and
placed my other one on his hip. I took a deep breath,
got down on my knees and tried to turn him over, gently,
quietly, but with force. I couldn't get the leverage.

I stood up and regrouped. I considered my options.
Turning him over was out of the question. I could either
peel his pants off or try to reach beneath him and get the
wallet out from between his ass and the cushion. Peeling
his pants off seemed like the easiest option until I realized
that I would have to cover my tracks. This wasn't twenty
dollars we were talking about. Actually, at that point, I
didn't know how much money we were talking about. But
I did know we were talking about a credit card and a
website that sold cock enhancers.

I reached between his ass and the couch cushion
and slid around until I found the bulge that signified his
wallet. I had a harder time getting my hand into the pocket

because it was buttoned and it required some contortions. I finally got it out.

I took the wallet upstairs with me rather than put it back and go through the whole process again when the time came to return to the card.

I woke up the computer. No reply. I opened the second email, clicked the text, clicked order. I took the Mastercard from the top of the stack in the first flap of the wallet. I filled out the required fields using my father's information to the best of my knowledge.

A three month supply of Cocksure for only three easy payments of $29.95, billed as C-sure.

I didn't know if that meant it took three months to work, or if it worked immediately but temporarily. Either way I had to get started right away. I ordered next day shipping figuring that if I was lucky enough that my father didn't notice the three easy payments of $29.95 on his billing statement, he wouldn't notice an extra $9.95 for shipping. If he did? Hopefully I would already have posed by then anyway.

I hit submit. I hit confirm. I put the computer to sleep. I ran back downstairs.

I said, "Dad." I shoved him. I said, "Dad."

I slipped the card back in the wallet. I got down on my knees. I slipped my hand beneath his ass and the couch and he shot straight up. He wasn't looking at me. He was facing forward. I left my hand where it was, tried to relax it, but my father's ass was heavy when he was sitting up, and it was cutting off my circulation.

I looked up and saw my father's head turning. It stopped when his eyes met mine. I got ready for the worst, but he didn't seem to recognize me. That was worse than the worst.

"Dad?" I said.

He just kept staring, as though I wasn't there. No, not as though I wasn't there, as though I wasn't me, as though I was something inanimate, or worse, something animate, conscious even, but without an identity, an I without a him or a me.

I jerked my hand out from under him, but he didn't seem to notice. There was no feeling left in it, but I didn't shake the blood back in. I just sat there with it on my lap, animate but lifeless.

My hand is to me as I am to my father.

"Dad?" I said, getting to my feet.

I stood up creaky and backed away slowly. My father was still staring into the space I'd displaced as I bolted up the stairs and into my room, slamming the door behind me.

It was a while before I realized that Maria hadn't shown up that night. Maria never showed up that night. I tried to tell myself that it was for the best, but I still had trouble falling asleep, and the sheep would only count up to three.

I woke up at noon the next day and my thoughts jumped straight to the pills. I knew they wouldn't be there yet, even though it was the next day, so my thoughts jumped to Maria.

I ran to the living room window, but there was no sign of life between my house and hers. There was, however, a car in front of Mrs. Malatendi's, a yellow Miata convertible with its top down to reveal a black leather interior. The color of the car insulted the scorched grass of the lawn beyond. It didn't really need mowing. In fact, mowing would be bad for it. I slipped on my shoes and ran outside.

I mowed slowly, in racetrack rings, looking toward the window always, risking the evil eye of Mrs. Malatendi in hopes of a sign of what had become of Maria and what it had to do with the car.

I got my answer as I was finishing up the front. Maria stepped out the door, her hand in the hand of a man maybe a little younger, or at least a lot more fit, than my father. He was wearing cutoff camouflage fatigues with sandals and a flannel shirt unbuttoned to the middle of his bald, chiseled chest.

The fatigues were what tipped me off. Maria's father.

I still didn't know whether to believe her version of

his life story, whether he was still dangerous, had ever been dangerous, but my need to talk to Maria overcame my fear and also my sense of propriety. I let the lawnmower sputter to a stop and went over to interrupt their reunion.

I didn't know what I was going to say as I stopped them on the path between the front door and the car. They didn't notice me until they were only a couple of steps away. When they saw me, they stopped and cut off whatever they were talking about. We made a very quiet triangle. Maria and I were awkward, Maria's father was puzzled, trying, apparently, to take my measure. She obviously hadn't told him about me.

I was talking before I even realized it, without having planned what I was going to say.

"I should be ready to pose nude for you in about six weeks," I said.

Neither of them responded with words. Maria's eyes popped open and she suddenly looked, with her surprised expression and her hand in her father's, like a little girl. In the time of their silence, the time I had to consider what I'd just said and to whom, her father just stood there with his brow furrowed. I would have expected him to be angry. He didn't look angry.

He broke the silence with a whiny voice.

"Do you really think the lawn needs mowing?" he said.

Of course the question was rhetorical. He was telling me that the lawn didn't need mowing, but I took it literally as an excuse to get away.

"You're right," I said, and ran back to the mower, pulling the cord and filling the front yard with its din, even though the front yard was already done. I went over the same patch of grass again and again as I watched them make their way to the car. I didn't go around back until they'd peeled out and turned the corner.

My father came home and went directly downstairs without a word. I didn't know whether it was a good sign or bad, whether he remembered the scene from the night before and was embarrassed or suspicious, or whether he was just particularly tired. I figured it was best to wait and see.

I had enough cash from mowing the lawn that I could order in, but I decided I should hang onto it in case my father figured out what I'd done and made me pay for it. I ate the leftover chicken cold because chicken is even more disgusting from the microwave.

Maria didn't come over again that night, and the Miata didn't return before I fell asleep.

The car was there, though, when I woke up late the next morning. I ran out to the mailbox in nothing but my pajama bottoms to see if the Cocksure had arrived yet.

There were a few bills, a couple of circulars, and a package wrapped in brown paper crammed into the mailbox. I ran back to the house, dropped everything but the package on the kitchen counter, went to my room, and slammed the door behind me. I looked the package over. It was unmarked except for my father's name and our address —both handwritten, scrawled—postage and postmark. No return address, no logo, nothing to suggest who or what my mother and I were dealing with. I peeled the package open, careful not to tear the paper in case there was something important inside, instructions for use or a note from my mother. The wrapping was thick and layered. I unraveled a section of it longer than me. When I finally got to the end, I found nothing but ten blister sheets, each containing nine little blue pills.

There were no directions, but I figured if ninety pills equaled a three month supply, that worked out to one per day. I decided to take one right then, and then another at the same time every day. I didn't know whether to take it on a full stomach or empty, with water or milk. I figured empty was safer, so I swallowed the pill with a glass of water. I waited for something to happen.

I didn't feel any different, but I went and sat on the bed for maybe an hour before I decided that the effect must not be immediate. After that I collected the packaging paper and shoved it to the bottom of the kitchen trash can, beneath the chicken bones, the greasy skin bits and gristle.

Then I hid the pills in the box of art supplies and went to check my email. No reply. I opened the email from my mother and hit reply.

I typed:

> Mom,
>
> I received the three months' supply of Cocksure in the mail today. Here's hoping that it grows my cock up to three inches, and that Maria comes back to see it.

I hit send, wondering if Maria would come back to see it. I thought back to the last time she'd disappeared. That had lasted exactly two days. She'd been gone two days again, but this time she wasn't visiting her father. This time her father was visiting her. Or else he'd returned for good.

At that point I was sure she'd come back sooner or later, so I had to be prepared. My cock hadn't grown at all, not that I'd expected it to by then, but I decided to kickstart the process with another one, just this once.

I swallowed the pill without water or food and put the rest back in the box. I removed some pencils and my sketchpad and laid them out on the floor to make it look like I'd been working on my masterpiece all along. I thought about actually working on it a little, to be more authentic, but it didn't seem like it could be authentic without Maria, or at least Jane Grundy, so I went to lay down on the living room couch.

But lying on the couch wasn't as satisfying or numbing as it usually was. I couldn't shake that notion, that doing my own thing didn't seem authentic without Maria or Jane Grundy. Maria, of course, was out of the question, at least for the moment. Jane Grundy, on the other hand—there was really no way of knowing, not without a call.

I wouldn't have called her if I hadn't had a reason, but I did have a reason, a good one, a question, and the answer could go a long way toward explaining my situation. I wanted to ask her what she'd told Maria when she'd called. I couldn't think of anyone else, besides Maria, who might have an answer.

I knew the number by heart. I'd never called it, but I'd heard it repeated a number of times nightly all summer. I didn't know, though, about the etiquette. She was never on the air during the day. I knew because I'd awakened to the white noise of pure waves, save for the occasional glitch of overlapping AM frequencies, in the haze every morning. And some lonely afternoons I'd switch on the radio just in case, in hope that I was wrong.

That part, at least, was positive. I wanted to call her when she wasn't on the air. I was terrified of the possibility (whatever the probability, as long as there was any) that I would call for an answer and get pity instead. Not from Jane Grundy—never as long as I'd been listening. From the audience, if anyone else listened like I did. Maria and I had never talked about that.

Day was the only time you could be sure she wasn't on the air. Sometimes, even at night, or when night was slipping into dawn, when it seemed like she'd already signed off and I'd fallen asleep to her or to the static, I'd be jolted awake by a sudden yelp of feedback as she went live, and the sound of her cartoon voice.

Those nights it was hard to fall back asleep at all.

But, then, what about her own sleep?

Even off air, I didn't want to risk incurring her wrath for waking her from the sleep that she was so generous as to provide for anyone else who was listening. I guess I just had to. I picked up the telephone, and dialed.

It seemed to take forever. I lost count around eleven but kept listening to the rings, as though they'd been what I was after in the first place. By the time the ringing stopped, I'd forgotten what I'd been calling for.

"Hello," said a voice.

It was a woman's voice, an old woman's voice to guess from the shake and the timbre of it, tired too, as if it's person was exhausted from climbing the stairs to the phone or had just been wakened by a phone that wouldn't stop ringing. But it didn't sound like Jane Grundy's voice.

I remembered that I'd meant to call Jane Grundy.

"Jane Grundy?" I said.

"What's that?" said the voice, a little louder than before, and louder now, "A little louder."

I got out, "I wanted to speak," before she shouted "Louder."

That was the voice I knew, a voice that managed to squeak and squawk at the same time. I was so pleased with myself that I considered my mission accomplished.

I practically screamed: "Jane Grundy!"

"Never heard of her," she said, back to being a tired old lady.

I didn't buy it, and not just because I was sure I'd recognized the voice when it shouted, but because she'd denied having heard of Jane Grundy so quickly. Old people's brains don't work that fast, except Jane Grundy's.

"Liar," I said, shrill, "I can tell."

"You can tell what?" she said.

I tried to calm down a little. I didn't want her to hang up on me. I clenched my teeth.

"I can tell that you're Jane Grundy," I said.

There was silence on the other end, and for a second I thought I'd finally gotten through to her, that she was going to admit it, that she was going to let me get on with whatever I was calling about, which, at the moment, I couldn't recall.

"Louder," she said.

"I can tell that you're Jane Grundy!" I screamed.

Another silence, this one followed by a click and a dial tone.

At first I was furious in a way I couldn't remember having been before. It was my first ever hangup, mostly because I hardly ever had any cause to talk on the phone. I lifted it over my head as though to slam it into the receiver, but it never really went beyond that. A calm came over me just as suddenly as the anger had, maybe more, because it was so unexpected, even unjustifiable.

Either way, there it was: a convenient sort of peace and understanding. I realized it was good I'd been hung up on. Maybe I had had the wrong number. Even if I hadn't, I couldn't remember, wouldn't have remembered, what I'd ever meant to ask.

I put the phone back in it's cradle, and collected myself.

What had I wanted?

I couldn't remember. The thoughts flew through my brain so fast they were practically static, as in still, as in off the air. I hardly even noticed my body carrying me back over to the couch in the living room, laying me back down, putting me to sleep.

I didn't feel any different when I woke up, brain or cock, but I looked out the window and the yellow car was still there. That seemed like a cause for hope.

It was dark out by then, so I was surprised to find that my father's car wasn't out there either. I ran downstairs to see if maybe he had gotten home from the pharmacy some other way, but as I descended the stairs, I could already tell that the television wasn't on, and the empty couch was just a confirmation of my expectations.

I ran upstairs and checked the answering machine. There were no messages. I was a little worried about my father's whereabouts, but I was more worried about whether Maria might be coming over. My cock didn't feel any different than it had that morning, than it ever had, but my head felt light, the result, I assumed, of getting up suddenly from another long nap.

I went into my room, leaving the door open behind me so that Maria would know I was there if she came looking. I tried to work on my drawing, but I couldn't seem to get anything going. Everything felt the same. Everything felt exactly like it had before the Cocksure, before Maria, but after my mother's death. I took the blister sheets from

the box and looked them over. Nothing changed in my
pants. I popped a pill from its packaging, plunked it into
my mouth, and bit down hard. The taste was sweet, then
bitter. I kept crunching as the crumbs coated my tongue,
my teeth, my throat. Some of it made it all the way down,
the rest made my mouth dry and thick. When I opened
and closed it, it made that crackly, sticky sound that Mrs.
Malatendi's made when she got particularly worked up. I
could feel a foam of pill and saliva at the corners where my
lips met.

At that moment, everything started to feel different,
not just in my head or my cock. My whole body felt like it
was floating in space. I let the pill sheets fall to my bed
and removed my shirt, my pants, and my underwear slowly,
in order to savor the experience of becoming naked, and
because I wasn't sure that I could keep my balance if I
went any faster.

I stood in front of my full-length mirror and stared
at my pale, bald self. Nothing looked any different than
before, but I could feel it: something, change, radiating
from my crotch, through every inch of my body, warming
the solids and filling the hollows, pulsing through my veins
like little orgasms with every lubdub of my heart, and
hovering around me like an aura, but almost tangible. I
waved my hands through it like earth through ether, and
my fingers came away misty with it.

I could feel everything—the cold air exhaled from
the vents in the floorboards, the dust motes in the ducts

singing like stars. I heard the electricity radiating from my lamp and the echoing thud of my father's footsteps on the carpeted stairs, his voice calling my name from the end of a long metallic tunnel. And then I saw him standing in the doorway behind me, like the mirror was eyes in the back of my head.

The dark circles under his eyes no longer signified exhaustion, weariness, misery. They were beatitude, only there to contrast with the glow of his eyes, his skin. His voice filled the room, gently entering my body through every pore.

"What's this?" he said.

He held something up, let it dangle from his right hand. It swayed in the breeze of the air conditioning and his energy, and it took me a long time to make it out. The brown paper wrapping, fully unraveled, crinkly, smeared with grease.

I smiled at his reflection in the mirror. I didn't know if he could see me, his face didn't show it, but he took a step toward me, another, until he was directly behind me. He put a hand on my shoulder, and I continued to stare into the mirror as at a portrait—loving father, disheveled but stoic after a long day of work, nearly pubescent son, naked except for socks.

My vision blurred with tears.

My father said, "Is everything okay?"

He broke the pose, looked around the room. When his stare fell on my bed, the wrapping paper fell to the floor.

"What the fuck is this?" he said.

I didn't answer. He was a pharmacist, so I knew that if he took a closer look, he would recognize it for Cocksure. He took a closer look, let his arm drop from my shoulder and back to his side. He picked up the top sheet, the one with three pills missing or six pills left. I could sense his recognition.

"Where did you get these?" he said.

"Mom," I said to the mirror.

I don't think he took it as an answer. He turned me to face him and tapped my face, trying to snap me out of whatever he thought I was in. He waved the sheet in front of my face saying: "These are warfarin," saying: "They're blood thinners," saying: "Who gave you these?"

"Mom said they grow your cock up to three inches," I said. "Results not typical."

He slapped me harder. He took me by the shoulders and shook me, the sheet of pills in his right hand scraping my skin.

I reached out and put a hand on his shoulder. I told him: "It's okay, Dad. Mom sent them."

He let go of me and slumped to the bed. He put his head in his hands. Then he jumped up suddenly, startling me. I almost fell over. He ran out of the room and I heard him rummaging through cabinets in the bathroom.

I made my woozy way down the hall and dropped into the chair in front of the computer. I woke it up. No reply.

I opened the second email from my mother as my father approached me from behind. He held a Dixie cup full of some translucent amber-colored liquid in front of me from over my shoulder.

"Drink this," he said.

But I didn't drink it. I didn't even take the cup. I pointed to the screen, to the sender's address, and said, "look."

He took his time reading it, probably over and over, considering how few words there were on the screen.

"Spam," he said.

But I heard the pop of the blister sheet, the pat of his hand against his lips, the click of the little pill against his front tooth, and the gulp as he swallowed it dry.

After that, the emails started coming more often, and we ordered everything my mother offered. Computer software, herbal remedies, pornography. They brought us, somehow, closer together. We were still always tired, and we didn't talk much more than we had before, but we were together, in the morning, before my father left for the pharmacy, when we took our horny goat weed, our Saint John's Wort, our off-brand Oxycontin, and in the evening, when we cooked dinner in the standalone rotisserie or Eggwave, popped some Canadian Zoloft, and settled down to watch a grainy dubbed and re-dubbed white-label snuff film.

My mother's messages never got any more personal, and her grammar was getting worse and worse. Now there were numbers slipped into the middle of words, random sentences cribbed from the classics, alphabetical lists of B-list celebrities, no longer celebrated and mostly forgotten.

For a while I studied them closely, as though they were in code, as though my mother was trying to tell me something in secret, something that they, whoever they were, didn't want me to know, but eventually I had to admit that my mother was rotting fast, that sooner or later her messages would be indecipherable, and then they would stop altogether.

We accepted her offer of a mortgage even though her life insurance policy had covered the first. We refinanced. We took out home equity loans. We made plans to visit a time-share condominium in Bermuda in January. Hardly a few hours passed without some kind of offer. My father left the credit card beside the computer when he left for the pharmacy.

Ordering and clicking refresh took up a lot of the time that I had previously spent sleeping in and laying around napping, but summer was still only half-through, and I had time to spare. Maria hadn't been over since the night she called Jane Grundy, nearly three weeks. I'd caught glimpses of the Miata peeling away from Mrs. Malatendi's house in the afternoon, seen Maria's father carry her slumped, sleeping body to the front door late at night. For a long time I told myself that the novelty would wear off sooner or later, that eventually she'd want to spend time with someone a little closer to her own age, or at least come back to get her art supplies. There was the matter of the portfolio, art school.

In the meantime, I continued to work on my own portfolio. I finished the crucifixion of the stuffed lamb more quickly than I'd planned to, because I occasionally forgot why I'd meant to delay in the first place, and by then I'd lost track of whether my cock was growing or shrinking or the same as it ever was. I moved on to a series of joyful mysteries with my memory of Maria as the virgin.

Eventually, though, my craft became too sophisticated for drawing on the floor, my oeuvre too large for my bedroom, and I realized that even though things were getting better between my father and me, and he seemed more hopeful, if not happier, he was still sleeping on the couch in front of the television. I turned the master bedroom into my studio.

But even my art couldn't kill all of the time. There were still the sleepless nights spent listening to Jane Grundy and counting increasingly deranged sheep, the odd afternoons when my mother seemed to be short on merchandise, the evenings when we had nothing left to shove in the convection oven, and my father was too weary to order pizza.

I missed Maria.

Not enough that I was ready to risk making another fool of myself in front of her father. And I knew that I wasn't going to get anywhere with Mrs. Malatendi. I did have her art supplies, but if I brought them back, and someone beside Maria was there to accept, I wouldn't have any more leverage. And then there was the fact that I had come to depend on those art supplies. My mother, curiously, hadn't offered any.

On one particularly empty afternoon when the Miata was out front, with nothing to order and without inspiration for another drawing, I went out into the oppressive heat and mowed half of Mrs. Malatendi's front lawn in a longitudinal pattern, left the mower sitting there in the middle of the yard, and went back across the street to my house.

I checked my email, but there were no offers. Then I stationed myself in the big picture window and waited to see what would happen.

About half an hour into my vigil, Maria's father stuck his head out of Mrs. Malatendi's front door and looked around, then went back inside. Ten minutes later he stepped out, shirtless, in short-shorts and a pair of moon boots, went over to the lawnmower, and started it up. I watched him finish the front lawn, glistening with sweat. He seemed to be tanning before my eyes. When the front was done, he went around back. I heard the mower running for another half hour, but he never came back around. He must have gone in the back door.

Still no Maria, and no good way of getting to her.

That was when I suddenly remembered what I'd wanted to ask Jane Grundy when I'd called her a while back. I ran into my studio, tore a sheet from the sketchbook, grabbed a stick of charcoal and scrawled:

"What did you say ~~when Maria~~ to the girl who called you about should she ask her ~~boyfriend~~ friend to pose nude for her???"

I placed it on the desk directly beside the telephone, switched on the desk lamp to illuminate the page, read the sentence over again and again in my head and then aloud, trying to make it sound natural, earnest, but the more I repeated it, the harder it was to skip the phrases I'd struck.

Maria was the girl. I'd wanted to be her boyfriend. I'd even been willing to pose nude for her. I was staring to worry that Jane Grundy had told her to get away from me, to never come back.

I wondered how my cock was doing. I hadn't thought about it in a while, though I'd continued to take the Cocksure, or warfarin as my father had called it, religiously, maybe fanatically, along with everything else.

I unbuckled my belt and peeled my pants and underwear away from my waist, looking down into the shadows. I was sweaty despite the intensity of the air-conditioning. I couldn't see anything. I slid the lamp toward the edge, toward my crotch, and pointed its beam down into the cavern of my pants.

It was barely there. But it wasn't the Cocksure or the Oxycontin, the calcium supplements or the estrogen supplements. Enough of those things tend to cancel each other out. I made a note to double up on yohimbine for the next couple of days. It was the nerves. I was all a-shrivel thinking of Maria, of how to solve the problem of Maria, of trying through Jane Grundy. It was almost dusk, so I had to get moving.

I had enough presence of mind to know that I'd never get the sentence out right without rewriting it. I ripped another sheet out of the sketchbook, placed it beside the previous, and wrote, slowly, neatly, with frequent glances at my model and an eye toward editing:

"A young woman called you a few weeks back about whether she should ask her male friend to pose nude for her. I was wondering how you answered."

It was concise. It was reasonable. It was perfect. I couldn't imagine anyone, not even Jane Grundy, denying such a logical request for information. Even better, it didn't sound pathetic at all.

I read it aloud and it sounded just like it had in my head.

I picked up the phone and dialed, fast, hoping to take care of my business quickly, before my confidence disappeared, but my fingers weren't cooperating. They fumbled across the keypad. I clicked, released, got another dial tone, took a deep breathe, and dialed again, this time slowly, as though performing a calculation.

I got an answer after the first ring, and before whoever was on the other end could even say hello, I was saying "What did you say when Maria to the girl who

called you about should she ask her boyfriend friend to
pose nude for her?"

There was a long pause, and then a man's voice said
"Excuse me?"

I knew I had screwed up my delivery, but it wouldn't
have mattered anyway. I hadn't prepared for, hadn't even
considered the possibility that a man, that anyone but Jane
Grundy, could answer my call.

Before I could find an answer, if you can even answer
"Excuse me," I heard a voice in the background. I couldn't
hear what it was saying, but whatever it was saying, it
was saying it to the man on the phone, and he answered:
"Some pervert talking about getting naked with…"

I slammed the phone in its cradle before he could say
anything else.

The next morning there were no emails. That hadn't
happened since before the Cocksure, and it made me
nervous. I went over to Mrs. Malatendi's. The car was there
again. I found the mower in the back yard. The lawn was
clean-shaven, the lines as clear as they'd been the day
before. I started the mower and began with the back.

When I'd finished with the whole lawn I was soaked
with sweat. I went back inside without collecting payment
and went to bed without checking my email, without
showering or even changing out of my grass-stained
clothes, without any real hope that Maria would ever be
over with my money.

There were no offers again the next day. I realized it was time to have a talk with my father, but he was already at the pharmacy, so it would have to wait. I went across the street to Mrs. Malatendi's.

The lawn was worse than short, it was scorched-brown and dead looking. I started the mower and did the whole yard in a racetrack pattern, digging up huge clumps of dirt with every pivot. By the time I was finished it looked more like a desert than a lawn.

I went to the door and rang and rang and rang the bell. I was still pressing the button when the front door opened inward to reveal Maria's father. We were separated by the storm door, and it was only then that I caught my reflection in its plexiglass. I didn't look good. I was sweaty and dirty, and my eyes seemed to be rolling around in their sockets like a broken baby doll's.

Maria's father opened the storm door gently, and I took a step back.

He said, "Are you okay?"

I said, "I've mowed the lawn two and a half times in three days."

He stuck his head outside, looked around.

"I don't think it needed it," he said.

I said, "Is Maria there?"

He reached into his back pocket and pulled out his wallet. He fumbled around inside nervously, pulled out all the cash inside—seventeen dollars—and shoved it toward me.

"Here," he said. "No more mowing."

I took the cash. I said, "Is Maria there?" but before he had a chance to answer I said, "I have her box." I said, "Tell her I have her box."

I shoved the money in my pocket and ran across the street, back into my house. I woke up the computer. No reply. I hit reply.

I typed: "Mom?"

I typed: "Mom, you haven't offered us anything in two days."

I typed: "Are you still there, Mom? Or did you finish rotting?"

I typed: "Please, mom. One last thing? For Dad."

I hit send.

I popped a Cocksure, a Xanax, two or three B-12 supplements, and reminded myself to talk to my father before I passed out.

My father came home that night and started to slice up
a can of cranberry sauce with a Ginsu knife my mother
had sent, not the sauce, but the can itself, just because he
could.

"Look at this," he said, slicing, slicing. "The can
doesn't stand a chance."

He was more animated than usual, and I could
tell that it was because he'd noticed that the offers from
my mother had started to trickle off, that he hoped they
were just trickling off, rather than stopping altogether.
I stood behind him in the kitchen, oohing and ahhing
appreciatively, trying to figure out a way to tell him that
his worst fears appeared to be true. But I couldn't find a
way to say it. I was holding out hope that my plea might be
answered, so I watched him slice up a can of corned beef
hash, some wax beans, asparagus, and choked down the
feast, trying to smile between bites.

But my father kept cutting. He sliced oranges clean
through with a single chop. He savaged a head of lettuce.
When he took out the new Teflon frying pan we'd received
from my mother a few days before and started sawing
through the space-aged polymer handle, I finally got fed
up.

I had to do something, but there was nothing I could do with him. The fact was, my mother had not been in touch in days, and I didn't want to talk to my father about it just then because I was just as worried as he was in my own way.

I left the table without asking to be excused, without a word in fact, and as I backed out of the kitchen, I noticed that my father didn't seem to have noticed. He'd made it through the handle and had started on the pan itself. It was giving him significantly more trouble. There was sweat standing out on his temples despite the chill, and he grunted with each thrust of the knife, and though there were shavings flaking off onto the counter and sticking to the vegetable and fruit smeared blade of the knife, the only tangible result of his efforts was a hot metallic smell that seemed to blend into the smell of him. In fact, it seemed like it had been missing before, that it was only natural now, and it was frightening.

I got scared he would suddenly notice me trying to slip by him, and maybe it was irrational, but I didn't feel safe. I spun one-eighty, ran out of the kitchen, down the stairs, and outside.

The air was still warm and thick despite the time. It was like the world never gave itself the chance to cool off anymore, like night was as good a time to broil as any, and I breathed deep to try to accustom myself to a drastic change in atmosphere I hadn't expected.

I forgot about the fire ants and sat down on the stoop. It was hard not to think about Maria, harder not to stare absently into the windows of her grandmother's house. The lights were on, but I couldn't see anyone or any sign of anyone—no shadows cast long on walls, no blinking blue television glare.

I made a point of looking away, turning my head to the right, up the street toward the empty life of my neighborhood, but my thoughts stayed with Maria, and my eyes made their way back to her too, or at least to her house. So I was staring again into her lit windows when a flicker in the corner of my eye gave me the impression that something was moving nearby. I turned in time to see Joel Danes and Barry Russell coast past me on their bicycles, but not in time to give them a wave, which wouldn't have been returned anyway even if it was noticed.

I gave up on the very idea of getting my mind off of Maria, but I had to do something to keep myself from staring stalker-like into her house. The only thing I could think of was to get up and walk. I counted to thirty, so it wouldn't seem like I was following Joel and Barry if they'd happened to stop just around the corner to do one of their stupid bike tricks or to examine some fresh road kill with sticks, then got up and walked off in the direction they'd gone.

They hadn't stopped, at least not before the horizon, so I had the whole neighborhood to myself. Sure, there were people nearby, awake even, eating and talking and arguing and watching television, but we were separated by vinyl siding and the desire to be separated from each other. It was lonely, but it was a sweet loneliness.

I sweated heavily as I walked, though I wasn't exerting myself all that much. I barely noticed it getting darker as I walked by the elementary school I'd attended. For a second I thought about going out back to the old playground, seeing how high I could get on the creaking, rusty swings, but then thought better of it, remembering rumors of older kids conducting their dark and sexual and possibly satanic rituals in the field behind the school. Before I'd really decided not to, I was past.

I kept walking. The moon was huge and hazy in the cream-black sky. When I got back to myself, to my surroundings, I was on the outskirts of the excuse for a city we suburbed. I was a long way from home and it was getting late, but I had no desire to turn around while there was still a chance my father was on the warpath in the kitchen. I kept going. My feet weren't tired.

I walked by a strip mall, a self-storage facility,

another school, this one outside my district. I'd been this
way before, but only in my father's car, and so everything
seemed somehow larger than I remembered, and there
was more of it, details missed in the blur and the glare
of windows. There was a sandlot on my left that I'd
never noticed before, maybe because I was always in the
passenger seat on my way into town and too tired on my
way back. There was a pay phone standing alone on the
corner beside the sidewalk, as though once there had
been something there, some reason that anyone might have
wanted to make a phone call from that spot.

At first, that was all there was to my interest. I
walked over to it, wondering whether it still worked,
whether anyone still even used pay phones anymore,
whether anyone could use that one. As I got closer, I could
see by the light of the nearby streetlamp that the receiver
was still connected to the phone. All the hardware was in
place. I lifted the hard plastic and examined it for grime,
but it seemed clean, though smudgy enough to show
that someone had in fact had it against his or her skin
sometime since the last rain.

I could hear the dial tone from there, but I put it to
my ear and listened to its hum for a while. It took me back
to the last time I'd heard a dial tone, the last time I'd tried
to call Jane Grundy.

I wondered what time it was.

From the look of the sky and the emptiness of the
street, it was late, but how late I didn't know. I didn't wear

a watch, and this was before kids with cell phones, at least in my town. Jane Grundy rarely went on before eleven, but usually it was closer to midnight.

I wondered how close it was to midnight.

And then I decided it didn't matter how close it was to midnight. If I called the number and she wasn't on yet, if whoever answered wasn't Jane Grundy, or denied being Jane Grundy, it wouldn't be the first time. If she was on, she'd never be able to trace the call back to me through a pay phone in an abandoned sandlot on the outskirts of the city.

I reached into my pocket and felt around for a quarter, but I only had fifteen cents in my pocket. I looked around the area lit by the streetlamp, scraping the sand with my sneakers. I found a dime and two nickels. I only picked up the dime because I thought that was all I'd need, and God only knows who'd had there hands on the change that ended up out there. I slipped the dime into the coin slot like it was burning my fingers. I followed it up with the dime and nickel I already had. I dialed the number as though automatically, and before it started ringing, a voice, half computer and half woman said, "You have five minutes."

One ring. Another. It picked up after the third and a voice that couldn't have belonged to anyone but Jane Grundy said, "Wait a god damn minute," and then there was a click, followed by another computerized voice telling me to please enjoy a selection of soothing music while I

waited, followed by music that was not soothing, not to
me. Classical or something. The changing keys and time
signatures always made me nervous.

I stood there kicking impatiently at the dirt around
my feet. I was starting to need to pee. The rival computer
voice, the first one, jumped in to tell me that I had three
minutes. The music became less and less soothing. I heard
voices, boy voices, Dopplering around the bend from the
direction I'd come, getting louder.

The phone clicked and Jane Grundy said, "So what
the fuck do you want?"

It caught me off guard, but it was more soothing than
the music. It was familiar. I said the first thing that came
to mind.

"Am I on the air?" I said.

"No," she said. "This is the abortion hotline.
Obviously your mother didn't take my advice."

In other words, we were on the air.

"You have two minutes remaining," said the
computer voice.

"What?" said Jane Grundy.

The bodies caught up to the voices from around
the bend. Two boys speeding toward me on bicycles. Joel
Danes and Barry Russell, I was sure, without yet being
able to make them out in the distance.

"It wasn't me," I said.

"Then who the fuck was it?" said Jane Grundy.

I was right. Joel and Barry.

"The payphone lady," I said.

I really had to pee now.

"Why in the hell are you calling me from a payphone?" she said.

"You have one minute left," said the payphone lady.

Joel and Barry were close enough to hear me now if I was too loud, if they noticed me at all. I lowered my voice, but didn't moderate my meaning.

"To find out what you told Maria," I said. "I mean, the girl who wanted her boyfriend to pose nude," I said. "I mean her friend."

"What the fuck is he doing out here?" said one boy to another.

They were hard to tell apart before dark, before puberty.

"Who wants to know?" said Jane Grundy.

"What the fuck are you doing out here?" said the other boy to me.

I pressed the receiver directly to my lips and whispered as loudly as I could, trying to at least keep it indecipherable to the boys who were now just feet away from me on the sidewalk, if it had to be audible at all.

"Am I posing nude or not?" I said.

Joel and Barry were walking toward me menacingly. I could feel the piss trying to force its way out. I clenched.

Jane Grundy cut out and the computer voice cut in: "If you would like to continue your conversation, please deposit twenty-five cents."

The boy's were almost upon me, still looking mean, but I wasn't scared. I'd just been hung up on for the second time in my life, the first by a computer, which didn't change the feeling at all. In fact, it made it worse. I was sure I'd been about to get an answer. I was sure that every second that passed made an answer, the possibility of ever getting an answer less likely. I needed to know who had fucked up. Me? Maria? Jane Grundy? I needed to know if I was ever going to get naked, big cock or not. I needed a quarter.

"Do either of you have a quarter?" I said.

The line went to dial tone before either could answer. Joel and Barry stopped short before I even lost it.

And I lost it.

I slammed the receiver against the cradle, the booth itself, my own head. I must have been crying because I could feel tears streaming down my cheeks, distinct from the sweat at my temples, my upper lip, the stinging in my eyes. I must have been screaming, too, because I didn't hear Joel and Barry saying whatever they were saying, hadn't noticed the change in their attitudes, from menace to fear to worry, until I felt a hand on my shoulder and I stopped swinging, finally exhausted.

"What the fuck?" said the voice attached to the hand.

I replaced the phone in the cradle, tenderly, as though to apologize for what I'd done, which, looking over

it, wasn't much, despite the violence of my intent. The
hand was actually rubbing my shoulder, but I didn't turn
around.

"Do you guys know Maria?" I said.

There was a pause, and then another voice, the one
behind my right shoulder, said, "From the bus stop?"

I rubbed the tears from my face, wiped my hands
on my pants, and turned to face them, my back to the
payphone as though it could protect me. I leaned against it
to appear casual.

"Did either of you ever pose nude for her?" I said.

I could see from their faces well before they answered
that they hadn't, that they were confused, and maybe, I
thought, a little jealous. Barry's answer proved I'd been
right about it all, the latter included.

"Are you kidding?" he said.

"She'd probably cut your dick off," said Joel. "That
whole family's crazy."

I don't know what they saw in my expression or how
I made it, but both of them backed off a step or two, and
Barry said, "Or maybe not."

I just stood there and they backed off a little more.

"I have to pee," I said.

The two boys stepped slowly toward their bicycles
without the usual attempt to hide the fact that they were
giving ground, retreating. I didn't acknowledge it. I walked
toward the far corner of the lot with my back to them
before they'd even made it to the sidewalk, though I was

probably walking funny.

I could sense them watching me as I unzipped, but I told myself that the Cocksure was working, although I couldn't really tell. I told myself that they couldn't see it anyway. I pissed powerfully and without hesitation. I heard the clank of a chain-guard against a chain as Joel and Barry peddled away.

When I was done, I zipped up and looked around. I was alone again, but this time it was kind of scary. I was a long way from home, at least on foot, and I didn't feel like walking. So I ran. I ran all the way home, as fast as I could.

I was breathless when I got home, and soaked in my own sweat. I collapsed on the landing, panting hard, almost choking, and lay there, curled fetal with my hands clutched to my stomach. I don't know how long it was before I felt good enough to get back up.

The kitchen was a disaster area. It seemed like my father had kept going a long time after I'd left, but at least the rest of the house was okay.

I switched on the radio. I was pretty well resigned by then to never knowing what Jane Grundy had said, but I wondered if my call had stirred up any trouble. It'd seemed like a long time since I'd been cut off, but when I thought back over it, it couldn't have been much more than half an hour. Jane Grundy could carry on about anything for half an hour if it struck her right.

But she didn't seem to be carrying on about anything at all. In fact, she seemed calmer than I'd ever heard her. There wasn't a single profanity in the entire first sentence after I turned it on, and even after that the cussing seemed almost half-hearted.

"Why didn't you call right away?" she said.

"I had to wait for my father to go to bed," said the caller.

I recognized the monotonous, bored sounding voice immediately, as though I still heard it every day, when really I hadn't heard it in weeks. Maria, on the air to crush my resignation.

"He was never actually my boyfriend," she said.

"You're fucking father?" Jane Grundy said.

She swore, but like I said, you could tell she didn't really mean it.

"No," said Maria. "The guy who called."

"What was he?" said Jane Grundy.

What was I? I didn't know, but she didn't either. I'd lost all hope of its meaning anything long before she managed to sigh: "He was just this guy."

"Guys," said Jane Grundy.

"Yeah," said Maria. "Guys."

They went on for a while, but they never said anything more substantial. It was almost like they were speaking in code. And really, they were. At least Maria was. I couldn't speak for Jane Grundy, and I couldn't imagine how anyone could manage to get her on their side, but it had happened. Maria had made it happen. Or Jane Grundy had let it—she was letting Maria let me go on the Jane Grundy show, letting her explain how it had been fun, but now her father was back and she didn't have time for kid's stuff any more, it was all art and family from here on out, how her father had found them a place, a faraway place, and how we had to grow apart, how it was natural, how he was going to call for her soon, as soon as he had set the place up with a room for her and a studio.

It was all bullshit. It was all Maria making herself feel better, and I couldn't believe that Jane Grundy was letting her get away with it. I switched off the radio, there didn't seem to be any end in sight. It was going strong.

That night I feel asleep without having to resort to the sheep. Something in me believed that I would get that last response from my mother in the morning, and for once, my body cooperated with that something.

But then something else, something in my dreams, had a darker or more real view of things.

In the dream, I was back to doing my art on the bedroom floor. I don't remember what it was I was working on, because in the beginning I was crouched over the sketchpad but staring straight ahead at the full length mirror. Something Jane Grundy was saying had caught my attention. I don't remember what, but it wasn't funny.

When I looked back down at the floor, that's all I saw. The floor. There was no sketchpad. I looked in my hands expecting to find a stick of charcoal, but there was no charcoal either. There weren't even any fingers. Both of my hands terminated in scarred stumps.

When I woke up, I wasn't frightened. I just knew that I would never see Maria again, and that if I wanted to continue my career as an artist, I would have to get my own supplies.

Congratu-
fucking-lations

The last email I ever received from my mother came the
next morning. The subject line was blank. The text read:
"Cut the crap."

   The sentence was jarring, but my relief was greater
than my disappointment. She'd gotten back to me, and it
was, after all, a full sentence, proper grammar, correctly
spelled. I didn't dare to believe that this would usher
in a whole new era of communication with my mother. I
assumed she'd mustered all of her energy, her decaying
bones, brain and spirit, to get it right this one last time.

   I waved the cursor over the text and it turned blue. I
clicked.

   Up came an order form, but there was no information
as to what was being offered. Just the usual fields for
name, address, credit card number, expiration date. My
father's card was still next to the mouse pad, right where
he'd left it, but I didn't need to refer to it any more. I'd had
all of the information memorized for weeks.

   I filled out the form and clicked confirm. I hit reply.

   I typed: "Thanks mom," and then I cried.

   But there was no time to wallow. I knew that this was

an ending, but also a beginning, a fresh start. I looked
out the picture window and saw something that I hadn't
expected to see, but should have—a big moving truck, and
Maria's father carrying a huge cardboard box toward it. I
considered going out and offering to help, but I was sure
that even if he accepted, I still wouldn't see Maria. And he
probably wouldn't accept.

I went into my father's bedroom and packed up
Maria's box as neatly as I could, filling it with everything
I hadn't put my own marks on, and slipping in a note that
read: "Thanks." I carried it into my room and placed it
on the floor because that was where she, or whoever she'd
send for it, would know to look.

I took my first shower in days. I put on a clean t-shirt,
some fairly fresh shorts. I reached into the still damp pants
I'd mowed the lawn in the day before and pulled out the
seventeen dollars of hush money, checked the rest of my
unlaundered clothes for cash, pulled up couch cushions
and checked under easy chairs. I had twenty-three dollars
total. I grabbed my Hudson Valley Savings and Loan
account book and glanced at my father's credit card. He
wouldn't notice, but this was something I had to do on my
own. I left the house and started the long walk to the mall.

I got to the mall sweaty, but invigorated. My body
barely registered the chill blast of air-conditioning as I
stormed the front entrance.

I went to the bank branch and closed out my account.
The teller tried to talk me out of it, told me don't you

want to go to college, threatened to call my father for confirmation. I dared him to. I even offered my father's number at the pharmacy. In the end, he just counted out the $211.13 that had been sitting in there all summer, muttering something about comic books and candy.

I tried my first ever I-am-an-artist-and-this-is-for-my-art stare, shoved the cash in a bank envelope, and headed for the stationary store because there was no art supply store in the mall or within walking distance.

I grabbed sketchpads. I grabbed watercolors and oil paints, Cray-Pas, pastels, crayons and colored pencils. I grabbed vine charcoal and poster board, construction paper, pipe cleaners and gum erasers. I filled one hand basket and a second and brought them to the register.

There was an old woman behind the counter. She gave me a benevolent look and said, "A young artist."

I nodded.

"Have you got enough money for all of this?" she said.

I nodded again, though I wasn't really sure. The pad of vellum alone was priced at forty dollars, but I just reached for the envelope, handed it to her and accepted my change. I had one last stop before leaving the mall.

The Sixth Sense was still playing, though not on as many screens. The signs still said it was rated R. There was just one guy at the ticket booth, probably the same one as before, but I couldn't say for sure—they all look pretty similar at that age, and I didn't get close enough, anyway. I wasn't about to try Maria's method for getting in free.

But I didn't have enough left over for a movie ticket, either, and I was still about as far from eighteen as I'd been earlier in the summer, so I just walked into the lobby without even pretending I meant to make the transaction.

No one seemed to notice. I hurried past the girl at the concession counter and headed down the hall I'd last walked with Maria. It was empty and dim and cold. I made it all the way to the end before I noticed that none of the Mylar signs in the hallway had said *The Sixth Sense.* I realized that they must have moved it to a smaller theatre on the opposite wing. But I hadn't really wanted to watch the movie anyway. My mother wasn't sending me messages through movies. They were just a tool. We communicated through emails, black market products, and toilet seats, I hoped.

I turned and headed back toward the women's room. There was no one around so I went in. The bathroom was empty too. I stopped at the stall I'd used before, dropped my pants and sat on the seat.

It wasn't warm. It wasn't cold, but it wasn't warm.

I wasn't quite ready to go home.

I looked up at the ceiling as though toward heaven, fiberglass tiles and a ventilation fan directly above my head.

I said, "Mom," and there was a quick cold reverberation off of the emptiness of the room. Before the echoes died, there was a rustling at the bathroom door. Then I heard it swing open and someone walk through.

I double-checked to be sure I'd locked my stall door, stood quickly and pulled up my pants. I climbed onto the toilet seat and squatted over it so that my head wouldn't stick out over the partition, placing a hand against each wall for support.

"Anyone in here?"

Yet another disembodied voice that I recognized, this one from Africa via death. It was Amos. I didn't respond, but I was surprisingly unafraid. I heard a mop bucket roll squeaky into the room. Its echoes off the tiles were beautiful and lulling, as was the slop of the mop in the bucket, the slush of it across the floor, the litany of cleaning sounds, the smell—chemical, dangerous, spotless.

I peered under the door, still squatting on the toilet seat, and saw a pair of black sneakers, heels facing me as a mop swayed side to side before the toes. The sneakers were as large as you'd expect from a man of Amos' height and bearing. He stepped forward, away from the door of my stall toward the row of sinks, and I knew I was taking a risk—there was a wall length mirror above the sinks—but I had to make sure it was Amos, the man I'd identified as Amos back at the beginning of summer, so I peeked my head over the top of the stall and looked.

His head was down, all concentration on the act of mopping, but in the mirror I could see the way his sad bright eyes stared out from his dark face. It was Amos, my Amos. He must have sensed me watching him because he lifted his head, but I got my own head back behind the orange metal door before his eyes met mine. Maybe he thought he was imagining things. The mop never stopped mopping. He didn't even take the time to look around.

He finished mopping the space in front of the sinks, and squeaked back toward the door. For a moment, I thought I was in the clear, but then I heard a stall door swing open and clack metallic against its wall. I realized he was starting to mop the stalls.

That was when I started to worry. He was going to make it to me sooner or later.

When he finished the first and moved onto the second, I thought about trying to make a run for it, but the floor was slippery, and it didn't take very long to mop a single stall, so I doubted I would be able to slip past unnoticed before he was out of the second and on to the next. I didn't know what would happen if he caught me, but I didn't want to risk it.

I decided my chances were better that he'd find my stall door locked and decide to come back later. By then he was in the stall next to mine, and I could have looked over and watched him working away if I'd wanted to, but I didn't. I was scared.

It only got worse when he finished with that one and moved on to mine. His hand slipped over the top of the door, its long, skeletal fingers gripping the edge just a foot or so from my head. I could see the tips whiten as he squeezed and clench as he pulled back on the door. The top moved an inch or so but the lock held.

I tried to send him a message with my mind: Let that be that. It was stupid, but he was dead and who knew what the dead knew. He didn't let that be that. He tried again. Again a few times. I was getting kind of woozy, losing my balance. When he jerked again I slipped sideways and slammed into the wall. He was still struggling with the door, so he didn't notice.

I don't think it occurred to him that someone might be behind that locked door until he stood on tiptoes and peered over, meeting my eyes with his, because when he did, when he strained upward, looking exhausted from his struggle with the door and maybe with the eternity of death in general, he seemed completely surprised.

He just stood there looking at me, straining, off balance.

I climbed down from the toilet, slid the latch on the

door and opened it inward. For a moment, Amos continued to stand tiptoe as though the door was still between us. I found myself staring directly into his red-vested chest.

There was a nametag on that chest. It said Amos. I staggered backward, got tripped up by the toilet and landed on the seat. Maybe even I hadn't believed until then that it was really him, my first email correspondent, my first dead man.

Amos seemed finally to take in what was going on. He let his heels back down to the ground, bent toward me, and reached out for my shoulder. I cringed before he touched me and he pulled back.

"Are you okay?" he said.

"Amos," I said.

I wasn't really responding to him, just saying something, anything, his name. I was thinking about his trying to touch me, whether he could have. In the movies, dead people are always transparent, and when you try to hug your loved ones your arms go right through them.

"Are you okay?" he said again.

I reached out for his hand, grabbed his fingers with mine, felt their scaly roughness against the soft tips of my own fingers, didn't let go.

"Are you?" I said.

This time he flinched a little, tried to pull his hand back, but gently enough. I just held on. He stood up to his full height and I held on. He took a step backward, and the mop fell over with a clack. The clack startled him and he kicked over the mop bucket.

The sudsy gray water spilled over the tiled floor with a splattering sound, pooled around our feet. We just stood there, his fingers in mine.

"I can feel you," I said.

"Are you okay?" he said.

"Are you dead?" I said.

His sad eyes got sadder.

"My mother's dead," I said.

He managed to get his fingers free. He looked around at the floor.

"I have to clean up," he said.

I knew what he meant.

I stepped past him, careful not to slip on the floor. He still hadn't moved when the bathroom door closed behind me.

I stumbled home like a drunk with three bags full of
supplies and a pocket full of spare change. The moving
van was gone and so was the Miata.

I checked the mailbox on the way in, but it was
empty. That was all right, I was sure something would be
along soon, and it was nice not knowing what it was.

I went into my studio. As I laid out my supplies,
I realized that I had forgotten to get a box like Maria's,
but then decided that it was okay, that I had nowhere to
take it all. When the studio was set up according to my
specifications, I went into my room to see if anyone had
been there.

Someone had. The box was gone. I could see, or I
imagined I could see, the faint impression it had left on
our carpet. But there was nothing else. No thanks, no
goodbye, no nice knowing you, no fuck off.

My father was borderline manic for the next three days.
It was obvious he'd realized the offers had come to an
end, but even as he started experimenting with the stuff
we already had—cooking handfuls of Ambien in the
crockpot, dismantling the DVD player with the all-in-one
handheld toolbox—I couldn't bring myself to acknowledge
that it was over. I kept my silence as a sign that I was
holding out hope, without telling him that we could count
on one more thing.

But that one more thing seemed to be taking its time
getting there.

I woke up early every morning to make sure I was
there just after the mailman came, but there was never
anything more than junk circulars and bills, both of which
seemed to have increased in volume since the spree of
offers and acceptances. Nonetheless, I opened every one,
standing out there beside the mailbox, particularly those
that came without recognizable return addresses, in hopes
that my mother had sent the crap-cutter.

She hadn't.

She hadn't.

She hadn't.

And the Miata was never there. The moving van

never returned.

On the fourth morning, I was waiting outside when the mailman rolled his little car up to the curb in front of our house. I stood there silent as he shoved a rubber-band wrapped stack of envelopes into the box and shut the door.

Before I even checked the contents, I asked him: "Is that all?"

"That's all," he said.

I stood on tiptoes trying to peak into the back of the vehicle. I could see the brown boxes stacked in the back, and I needed to be sure none of them were for me.

"No packages?" I said.

"That's all," he said.

It wasn't unkind, the way he said it. Maybe he knew something was up. He'd been our mailman as long as I could remember, after all. He must have noticed the sudden spike in packages that summer. Maybe he'd noticed the sudden decline too.

He drove off almost resignedly. That's the way it seemed to me. I wondered if there was anything I could do to be certain, in case the mailman wasn't honest, in case he'd noticed the spike and decided to take a cut for himself, a cut of the crap.

What cuts the crap?

I thought about jumping on the back of the vehicle and hanging on until I had a chance to get in there and see for myself. But I knew that it was a federal crime, tampering with the mail. It was a federal crime for me to tamper with the mail even if he was tampering with the mail.

There was no way I could prove it.

I walked back to the house, resignedly. At least that's the way it seemed to me.

It was always a surprise in those days, going back into
the house after checking the mail, even if I was never out
for more than five or ten minutes. Things had changed
so quickly after the decline of my mother. There were
new consumer appliances, and parts of new consumer
appliances in various stages of demolition, and pills and
pill crumbs scattered throughout the house, on the carpets
on shelves, tables, once-bare surfaces. The place was a
mess like I'd never seen, the kind you don't get used to.

My father was still going to work then, but I don't
know how well he was working. Not very well, judging
from the look of him when he left for the pharmacy.
And he always looked worse when he came home. I kept
waiting for the call that he'd been arrested for poisoning a
customer, like in *It's a Wonderful Life*.

The news kept insisting it was a wonderful life. My
father had it blaring that night as he sat atop the television,
firing the hypodermic needles full of insulin we'd ordered
from Mexico at a dartboard—I don't remember where it
had come from, except that it had come from my mother—
that he hadn't really mounted so much as propped against
the wall above the couch. When he ran out, the carpet
around the couch looked like certain alleyways I'd seen

on trips to the city, but my father didn't pick them up. Instead he cracked open a bottle of absinthe, took a great gulp straight from the bottle, ignoring the ritual of sugar and fire that the label romanticized, and spat it toward the target. The spray didn't make it anywhere near.

I smelled the licorice and alcohol burn over the stench of rotting food and technology gone wrong that was starting to be the smell of our house. The news said we were rich dot com, and our surround sound speakers rattled beneath the weight of my father.

I headed for my studio, but I didn't feel like doing art, and I didn't feel like listening to Jane Grundy. I had to figure out how to get things back to normal. If not the normal of the grand consumptive days, at least the quiet misery of early summer.

But how, if my mother was done with us, or done altogether?

I ran for the computer, woke it up. No response. I hit reply. I typed: "Mom?"

I typed: "What did you mean by cut the crap?"

I hit send, but I knew I had to try to figure it out for myself because my mother never responded directly, and these days she wasn't responding at all. So I asked myself what my mother meant by cut the crap.

Obviously not Ginsu knives. She'd already sent us some. And not crap. Nobody sells crap. Plus it's got to be illegal to send crap through the mail.

I googled "cut the crap" in quotes and got offers of

software, etymologies and some third-rate pop band. I ordered some of each, but I knew they weren't what I was looking for. I was going to have to go back out into the world for this one.

The mall wouldn't do. Too spread out, too many options, all too specialized. Nothing in the Pottery Barn, or even Williams-Sonoma could possibly cut the crap. Fortunately my father's pharmacy was located conveniently in the back of a Wal-Mart in the town across the river. It was too far to walk, so I hitched a ride with him the next morning, knowing that I could always check the mail when we got home.

I wandered the aisles all day, looking for something to cut the crap. Not patio furniture. Not family planning accessories. Not a rake or a hoe.

People were looking at me funny, people I might have known at one time, before my mother's death, before the orgy of offers. I didn't recognize any of them, but I recognized, through the opiate haze or the amphetamine buzz, the hunger, the terrible hygiene, that I might have recognized them once.

Nothing in the toy section. Not lamps or lampshades. Carpet squares can't cut the crap. Or mirrors. Please not the mirrors.

I could see why people were staring. Beneath the bright fluorescents suspended overhead, above their glare off the tile, I stood in the aisle of mirrors and stared my own self down. My clothes were filthy, my hair uncut and unkempt, my skin pale and blueish about the eyes, what looked like a crust of blood around my left nostril.

I stood there frozen until I ran. I ran until I bumped into someone in the hardware section, someone I might have recognized if I'd recognized her. She was motherly but not old, soft, warm-smelling, despite the sterile white labcoat she wore, a co-worker of my father's maybe.

She said, "Are you all right?"

"Just looking for my father?" I said.

"He's back in the pharmacy," she said. "Filling prescriptions."

She knew me, my father. I couldn't remember how.

"I'm on lunchbreak," she said. "Do you want to get some lunch?"

We sat in the cafeteria. The fluorescents there were just as harsh, but there were lamps above the fake wood tables. They added less light than sick, parodic ambience. There was a hotdog in front of me. Some fries, a small coke. Ketchup pooled on a napkin like blood in child's play.

"So how are you and your dad doing?" the woman said.

I took a big bite of my hot dog. I wasn't hungry but I didn't want to talk. I chewed longer than I would have normally, pointing at my closed mouth for a while to let her know. She finally gave in and answered for herself.

"I've been worried about you guys," she said. "Your dad's work is fine, but he seems sad."

I took another bite.

She said, "Or sick or something."

She had those kind of eyes that always look they're about to cry. It was pretty.

I swallowed. I said, "Do I know you?"

She went from near tears to a little laugh. Patronizing. I'd learned what it meant.

"I work with your dad," she said. "Remember? The Christmas party?"

Another bite. I felt the hotdog settling in my stomach.

It wasn't a good fit. She looked disappointed, as though my not knowing who she was was a flaw in her own personality.

"Maybe you were too young," she said.

I nodded, finished off the dog. We sat in silence as I chewed. I had to get back to looking. I thought maybe she could help.

"What do you think of when I say cut the crap?" I said.

She looked like she might cry again.

"I was just trying to help," she said.

But I didn't have time to explain myself. I felt like I was going to puke.

After spraying the gleaming white toilet with bits of over-chewed but undigested hotdog, I went back out to look. Now I had to avoid the pharmacy in the back along with the mirror aisle because I didn't want to have to face my father's coworker. I was too tired to explain what I'd meant about cutting the crap.

I must have wandered for hours, because by the time I made it back around to the front of the store, I could see that it was dusk outside. It was late enough in the summer that it was getting darker earlier, but it was late enough in the day that I knew I had to finish up quick.

I meant to work my way through the store one last time, methodically, methodically avoiding the mirror aisle, but I stopped in the first section I investigated.

Kitchen appliances. I couldn't imagine how I'd missed it before. My mother had sent us plenty of kitchen appliances and utensils. But never an electric carving knife. What could cut the crap better, or more thoroughly, more effortlessly, than an electric carving knife? I pulled it down from the shelf, set it on the floor, and sat down in front of it. I removed it carefully from the box, slipped the body and the blades from their separate bubble wraps, untwisted the tie and uncoiled the wire, assembled.

It was beautiful. It gleamed, sleek and dark, domestic and threatening. I was as certain that this was what my mother had meant as I would have been if it had arrived in our mailbox.

But it hadn't arrived in our mailbox. It hadn't arrived anywhere. It was just lying there in front of me on the floor of a Wal-Mart, a Wal-Mart that I didn't have the cash to get it out of. There was my father, but asking him to buy it would defeat the whole purpose. He wouldn't believe that my mother had sent it if he bought it himself.

Then there was his coworker, but no.

I slid the bubble wrap back over the blades, shoved the rest of the packaging back into the box, closed the box, and placed it back on the shelf I'd taken it from. Then I looked around. No one was watching. I shoved the whole thing—bubble-wrapped blades, handle, cord—into my pants, and hoped, as I felt the plastic of the wrap against my bare inner thigh, that the wrap stayed put, and barring that, that the Cocksure hadn't worked well enough to cause any trouble.

I walked slowly, because of the knife and because I was tiring, back to the pharmacy, to wait for my father, who I assumed must be getting ready to head home.

My father wasn't at the counter but his coworker was. She looked kind of frazzled. Maybe it was just that her hair had come loose from her pony tail, a few curly strands straggling at the edges of her face. She didn't seem to be holding my offenses against me anymore. In fact, I thought

I saw a little smile as she saw me, recognized me.

"Hey there," she said.

"Is my father almost ready to go?" I said.

She was suddenly very concerned, confused. She looked behind her, as though to see if my father was almost ready to go, but her answer proved she knew he wasn't.

"Your father left an hour ago," she said.

It wasn't surprising, but I didn't have a response for that. I didn't get a chance to respond anyway, because a hand grabbed my shoulder from behind, and the hand's voice, the voice of an older black man, said, "You caught him."

"Caught who?" said the woman behind the counter.

"This guy has something of ours," said the voice.

I turned my head and saw the store security badge, tried to think of something to say, but couldn't. The woman behind the counter did the talking for me.

"Oh that," she said. "I'm watching him for his father."

The hand didn't let go, but it let up a little.

"That doesn't mean he can steal from the store," said the voice.

"He isn't stealing," she said. "I told him he could pick out one thing. He must not have understood I meant I would buy it for him."

She was good, but I didn't know how good yet.

"A kitchen appliance?" said the security guard.

She broke composure for a second but regained it

fast.

"Well, I assumed he'd get a toy," she said.

"Whatever it is, it came from the appliance aisle," said the guard.

"I did say anything in the store," she said. "My mistake," and then turning to me, talking and looking at me like I was younger than I was, which was appropriate, which I appreciated: "What'd you get honey?"

I pulled the knife from my pants. The wrapping came off the blades as I did it, stayed in there. Luckily nothing got hurt, though later that night I noticed some frayed threads in the waistband. It must have looked kind of threatening. The security guard let go, stepped back. I turned around.

"Whoah," he said. "That's not a toy."

I didn't drop it.

"Me and my dad need it," I said. "For Thanksgiving."

The guard looked back and forth between me and the woman at the counter.

He said, "You're gonna buy it for him?"

"It's what he wanted," she said.

"Not very responsible," said the guard, delaying concession, but then: "At least put it back in the box."

The guard walked away. I worried that whoever he got next would get worse than he or she deserved, because I'd gotten nothing but what I'd wanted from the beginning, something to cut the crap. I couldn't help but crack a smile. Then I realized that I was probably still in trouble, with my father's co-worker, or with my father if he could be bothered with it. I forced my mouth closed and straight-lipped and looked up.

She was smiling. She wasn't trying to hide it. I smiled again. We just kind of sat there smiling at each other. I wanted her to call me something. Something I'd never been called before. Something like tiger or champ.

Instead she said, "I get off in an hour," and, "you better go get that box," which was just as good. I waved the knife at her and ran back toward the home appliances section.

It was getting dark as she drove me home. The carving
knife was back in its box, and the box was on my lap. I'd
thought, back in the store, about putting the knife that had
been shoved down my pants, pressed against my thigh,
back into the box and taking a new, unopened box instead,
but then I'd decided that the knife, that particular knife,
and I had been through something together, so I passed
the time of the drive by examining the imperfections of
the box, from where it had been jostled in shipping and
shelving, smudged by hands that didn't buy it, torn in
little places around the flaps by my opening and closing,
reopening and reclosing of it.

I caught her looking at me out of the corner of her
eye now and then, out of the corner of my eye, mostly at
stoplights.

I decided the damage to the box gave it character, as
though it had been sitting beside my mother in the spam
warehouse of the beyond, maybe even, at some point, used
to cut dead crap, and now it was being passed along to us
in one final touching gesture.

Of course, having gotten it at the store, I would never
be able to convince myself of that. I wondered whether
I would have been able to convince myself of it if it had

been delivered to my mailbox. I was hoping to be able to convince my father of both.

"You tell your father I'll see him tomorrow," she said.

I looked up at her and then out my window. We were in front of my house, the gear in park. I realized I hadn't felt the sensation of moving in a while. I wondered how long it had been.

"Yeah," I said, unbuckling my seatbelt.

"And take care of yourselves," she said.

She reached up to ruffle my hair as I was opening the door and leaning away to get out, so it was awkward for a second, and then I was outside the car, the door was closed, and she was driving off.

I looked up at the windows of our house. They were all dark. My father's car was in the driveway, which meant that he was home. The fact that he hadn't seemed to have missed me meant he probably hadn't stopped for food on the way home or ordered anything. I figured he was already asleep on the couch.

Still, I had to be thorough about things. I kind of slipped the box, which was clenched between my arm and my body, behind my back. Then I walked over to the mailbox and opened the door. As I slid the few envelopes, all bills and credit card offers, out of the hollow metal tube, I brought the box up to meet them. It wasn't exactly sleight of hand. Considerate of hand. It didn't matter anyway. I closed the door and walked toward the house.

Inside, the smell was worse than I remembered. This was partially because I hadn't been outside of the house that long since before my father's rampage. But it was partially because the smell had actually gotten worse. Things that had been rotting had continued to rot, and in the few hours that my father had been home without me, he seemed to have managed to add even more to it. The look was as bad as the smell once I got the landing light on.

The trail of mess had made its way out of the living areas and was trickling up and down the stairs. I was glad I'd found something to cut the crap. We were probably only a few days away from total loss by then.

I went upstairs, figuring it could wait until tomorrow at least, that is, at the latest, as long as my father was already asleep down there. But he wasn't. I didn't find out until I got into my studio. His bedroom.

"Where've you been?" he said.

It scared the shit out of me. I dropped the knife and the mail on the floor. When I bent over to pick them up, my head hit the doorknob on the way down. I stood back up rather than risk hitting anything else and switched on the light.

My father was sitting on the bed, fully clothed with

his legs spread out in front of him. He looked like a giant child. That room, at least, was clean, even if the smell of the rest of the house was seeping in through the doorway.

"Sorry for using your studio," he said. "The rest of the place was such a mess."

The way he said it kind of stunned me. It was like he didn't realize that my studio was his bedroom, that he was the one who'd made the mess.

"I'll start cleaning it up tomorrow," I said.

"What's that?" he said.

I didn't know at first what he was referring to. He wasn't pointing at anything. Still just sitting there on the bed with his legs out in front of him, his hands at his sides. I looked around for whatever he might be asking about, but there was nothing but the remains of the bedroom he'd shared with my mother and my art supplies, which he knew about, even if he wasn't really paying any attention. As my look made its way to my feet, it caught the pile of stuff in my arms and stopped.

What's that? It's an electric carving knife.

"I don't know," I said. "It was in the mailbox when I got home."

I walked it over to him, placed it on the bed between his legs. He looked down without much interest.

"An electric carving knife," he said.

"I didn't look inside," I said. "I don't know what's in there."

"It says electric carving knife," he said.

My father flopped backward onto the bed like a frustrated child. I lifted the box from the bed and set it down on his chest.

"Maybe it's from Mom," I said.

"Why would your mother send an electric carving knife?" he said.

"I'm tired," I said. "You don't even know if that's what it is."

My father lifted his head a little, like he was trying to see through the box to what was inside, but just ended by squinting then crossing his eyes. He let his head fall back to the bed, but then he lifted his arm and rested his hand on the box.

I hoped my plan would work, but I decided it might work better if I left the rest to him. I said, "I'm going to bed," reached out and touched his shoulder, and went across the hall to my room.

The sheep didn't even bother trying to make puns that
night, but they didn't have anything good to say either.
They lined up in two big groups, one on either side of the
fence, and shouted at each other for hours.

One side was screaming my father would never buy it,
would never even believe that I'd found a box containing
an electric carving knife in our mailbox, a box without so
much as a mailing address let alone postage, and that it
had somehow been sent to us by my mother. The other side
screamed that he would, that he would believe, because he
wanted to believe, but that when he went back into work
the next day, his coworkers, the woman who'd bought it
for me or the security guard, were sure to say something
about it, would ask why I'd wanted it, what I'd planned
to do with it, and not only would my father never stop
demolishing our home until it was rubble, he'd never trust
me again either.

The sheeps' ranting grew louder and louder until they
cancelled each other out, but it made their message all the
more clear: that nothing good could come of it.

I don't know how I ever got to sleep that night, but I did.
I got to sleep and I slept hard and late, and I didn't wake
up until, just before noon, I was jarred by a series of loud
clanks. At first I assumed it was my father, breaking more
stuff, but a glance at the clock told me that my father
should have been at work long before.

So I stayed in bed, afraid, as the clanking continued,
trying to imagine what the clanking could be. It kept
going, punctuated occasionally by a crumple, a crash, a
rattle. Too loud to be an animal. Too careless, I hoped,
to be a criminal. And Maria was gone, I thought, without
having made any noise louder than the shhh of her pencil
shading a page, the tiny, satisfying crunch of scissors
through heavy-bond paper.

The sounds came down the hall, getting closer,
through the open door of my bedroom. I hid beneath the
covers. Someone stopped in the doorway and stood there. I
could hear him breathing, the fabric of his clothes against
the doorjamb, then a cough, a fake one, the type meant to
stir a sleeping boy, my father's fake cough.

I slipped the cover from my head, my hands still
clutching the hem, my eyes peering over the edge like
Kilroy. My father was standing in the doorway brandishing

the electric carving knife with a huge grin on his face.

"Your mother sent this," he said.

My plan had worked. I slid the covers down to my chest, released my death-grip on the blanket, eased myself up by the elbows. But then I remembered that my plan had only half-worked, and that that could be worse than its not working at all.

"Why aren't you at work?" I said.

"I called in sick," he said. "This," he waved the knife from side to side, "called for a celebration."

I just stared at him, trying to figure out what he meant and wondering whether what he meant was good or bad. He didn't seem to notice.

"What am I saying, celebration?" he said. "I mean a whole new way of life."

There was nothing expressive about his voice or gestures. But I saw his face. I could see he meant it somehow, but I couldn't figure out how. I would find out over the course of the next week.

We started by cleaning the house. It took three days, that
first included, and my father called in sick each morning.
During that time, he almost never let go of the electric
carving knife. It became like an extension of him, so
that when he set it down, to help me right a largescreen
television he'd knocked over on one of his rampages, his
hand seemed naked, or worse, vulnerable. But not in some
abstract and poetic way. It seemed vulnerable to something
imminent, immanent, hiding beneath or behind the next
major appliance that needed repositioning or dusting off.

He would grab the knife tight again as soon as
anything was in its place.

We lifted, we tossed, we vacuumed, swept, scrubbed
and polished, and then, finally, we were done.

We celebrated by lounging around our spotless living
room, popping a Vicodin apiece, but only one because
we were running low, and sipping a glass of iced tea in
honor of Maria. At least I was drinking to Maria. No hard
feelings, I thought, as long as I didn't think too hard.

But I didn't think thinking was in order. I had
decided that with the house back in order, and my mother's
emails over, everything would go back to what had passed
for normal. Except that now I was an artist. School

would be starting soon enough, and when I got back, my loneliness wouldn't be the same any more. It would be the loneliness of someone born to it, for the purpose of observing and depicting what he saw, from the outside, through the filter of his own genius.

I focused my observation on my father's hand, the right one, dangling over the side of the armchair, still clenching the electric carving knife, its cord resting on the floor, the cord's twist-tie having come undone at some point in the last three days.

There was still the issue of what would happen when my father went back to work, when he spoke with his coworkers, but it didn't seem like such a worry now that the house was clean.

My father must have noticed me staring at the knife, because he took a last, deep gulp of his iced tea, set the glass on the floor, and sat up straight. I looked up into his eyes.

"Now," he said.

"Now what," I said.

"Now we figure out what to do with this," he said.

He stood up and walked into the kitchen. I sat there on the couch for a minute trying to imagine what, besides dismantling it and putting it back in the box, we could possibly do with it, then followed him in just in time to see him placing the knife on the counter.

It wasn't normal the way he did it. He didn't put it down like you put a knife on the counter. It was ceremonial, almost liturgical, with hand flourishes and head bows that didn't look at all funny. It was serious, and it was scary. I tried to cover.

"So, I guess I'll go find the box," I said.

My father spun to face me.

"Why?" he said.

I took a step back.

"To put it away?" I said.

For a while he didn't answer, but the way he reached behind his back, the way he touched the knife, protectively, the way he hadn't touched me in so long, was answer enough. And then the words. The words were too much.

"I am never letting this out of my sight," he said.

I told my father it should be our little secret, and that kept him quite for almost a week. Literally. For the last few days, he didn't open his mouth except to call in sick and maybe shove a little food in on the sly. He said we were fasting, but I never heard his stomach growl like mine.

Early on he'd told me he was going to quit his job, but I was there every morning to make sure that he said the right thing, that he was sick. I didn't know how long the whole ordeal was going to last, and I didn't see any point in his ruining his life over it if it could be helped. I hoped it could be helped.

It got to the point where he didn't leave the kitchen. Sometimes it was too much for me. I would look up from the knife and see a tear sliding over the rim of his eye

or dripping down his cheek. I couldn't tell if he was sad
or happy or if he'd just been staring a long time without
blinking. I'd look back, and suddenly I wouldn't be able to
remember what we ever saw in it, what I'd been trying to
see in it a minute before.

"Dad?"

He might have grunted. He might have said,
"What?" He could even have fumbled an arm out toward
my head and ruffled my hair or my shoulder or whatever
his hand came across, but he never turned my way.

"What are we doing again?" I'd say.

If he had his hand on me, he'd let it drop to his side.
It wasn't anger or disappointment. I think he just forgot I
was there. When he answered, his voice was flat, his tone
far away. Not robotic. It was like he was reciting his side of
some minimalist catechism.

"Watching," he'd say, "thinking."

That's usually where I left it, where I left him. I'd go
to his bedroom, my studio.

I snuck outside once or twice, but ever since the fire
ants on the stoop I hadn't been able to sit on it five minutes
without picturing my ass bit raw. In any case, it was late
and I didn't go outside at all on the night my father finally
gave in.

I was in my studio, scribbling away at a pietà without
really meaning to, using markers and colored pencils
on gray construction paper. I had Jane Grundy on, but
quietly. My father hadn't specifically forbidden the radio,

but I figured it was off-limits since we were fasting and spending most of our time watching and thinking. I slipped in and out of attention to her, to my art, to her, which is why I didn't find out that my father was giving away our little secret until a few minutes too late.

The knife was all out of proportion in my pietà, the size of Jesus in his mother's lap, when the real thing fit comfortably in my hand before my father stopped letting me touch it. He hadn't laid a finger on it himself after the first couple of days.

That was my train of thought as I searched out the perfect orange for the power switch, trying out several of my many markers and pencils on a piece of scrap paper I kept beside the masterpiece itself. By the time I'd worked my way into the crayons, I'd worked my way into wondering what good our little secret was if we never did anything with it, and finding the perfect orange didn't seem so important any more.

I was about to scrap the whole thing when Jane Grundy said, "Get on with it."

The caller said something, but whatever he said was obscured by feedback.

"Turn your goddamn radio off," said Jane Grundy.

There were a few more seconds of feedback, some fumbling, and the caller whispered: "Sorry."

"Fuck sorry," said Jane Grundy. "Last chance to dish."

I felt sorry for the caller. He was the second type, the

type that needed someone to talk to.

"Sorry," he whispered, sorry for being sorry. "I...
my family...we got a...blender."

There was a moment of dead air, unusual for Jane
Grundy's program. It helped to keep my attention even
though I didn't care one way or another about blenders. Or
as Jane Grundy put it, "I don't give a shit about blenders."

Another moment of dead air, during which the man
on the line was supposed to explain why she should give a
shit about blenders or why he gave a shit about blenders, or
something, anything, I guess, but the nothing he managed.

"You're wasting my fucking time," said Jane Grundy.

"Sorry," said the man.

The line went back to the dial tone, and Jane Grundy
went insane. She started screaming that nobody hung up
on her, she hung up on nobodies. Then she went on about
what happened to the last caller to hang up on her, and
from there to what was going to happen to this guy.

The rant was strewn with obscenities obscene even
for her, and I couldn't help but laugh. I laughed harder
than I had since that first time I'd heard her. Then she
said, "Hasn't this bitch ever heard of caller ID?"

I was still recovering as she dialed the man's number,
kind of hiccupping when I heard the ring on the radio
followed by the stereo tones of the phones in the bedroom
and kitchen. I froze at the second bedroom ring and
second kitchen ring respectively.

The caller wasn't answering. My father wasn't

answering. I bolted from the room as third led to third.

I found my father in the kitchen facing the phone. He looked like the guy in the movies who's been possessed by something bad, but the good in him is trying to fight the bad and do the right thing. The problem was, I didn't know which was the good and which the bad.

I said, "Dad?"

He didn't even notice. Either the good or bad was winning, and this was represented by a faint trembling in his whole body, like television static, almost imperceptible from a few feet away if it weren't for the sweat beading from the pores on his forehead and upper lip, trembling there in defiance of gravity. Fourth ring. Fifth.

I said, "Dad." I shook his arm. I said, "Dad. The phone's ringing."

He'd turned the kitchen radio off to hush the feedback. I turned it on. I turned the volume up as high as it would go and Jane Grundy said, "I can wait all fucking night."

My father returned, good or bad. At first he didn't move a muscle—it was all in his eyes. Then his arm shot out, and his hand switched off the radio before Jane Grundy could say another word, before the phone could ring a sixth time. A seventh.

"Leave it off," he said, but the machine picked up, and my father's voice told the neighborhood whose residence Jane Grundy had reached and that we were unable to answer the phone and that if she would leave a detailed message, we would call her back as soon as possible.

Her detailed message was: "Here's my detailed message: you won't need to call me back because I know you're not unable to answer the phone because I know you just called me and hung up on me and no one fucking hangs up on me or I keep calling back and back and back …"

My father pressed the stop button on the machine.

There was a moment of silence before the phone started ringing again. My father switched off the ringer and went back to the age-old struggle, immobile. I could still hear the one in the bedroom. Third, fourth, fifth.

I ran back toward the bedroom, intending to switch off the other phone's ringer, not sure if it was the right or wrong thing to do, just that it was what my father had done, but when I got there, Jane Grundy was practically pleading: "Just pick up the phone. I don't want any trouble. I just want to talk to you."

Sixth, seventh, message, dial tone. I reached out and switched off the ringer. I was walking across the room to switch the radio off as Jane Grundy began to dial again.

She said, "I'm only going to try one more time. I've got a show to do. People depend on me to put them to sleep. But I think we'd all like to know a little bit about your blender."

The phone on the radio rang. The one in my father's room was silent, but still I felt it calling me, offering me the chance to make peace with Jane Grundy, to defend my father's honor. It was the battle between good and bad, and I didn't know any better than my dad.

Ring. Ring. Jane Grundy practically whining: "Now you're just being mean," saying: "Tell us about your blender."

"It's not a blender," I said.

I tore the phone away from my face and stared at it as it rested almost innocently in my palm. I had no idea how it had gotten there, to my ear, my mouth. Fortunately, I'd caught Jane Grundy off guard. The phone and the radio called to each other from across the room, quietly at first, but with increasing intensity. Jane Grundy snapped out of it and into the phone.

"Turn your fucking radio off," she said.

I snapped out of it and toward the radio. The phone cord stretched and snapped from my hand, backward and toward the floor. Jane Grundy was demanding what the fuck was going on in ascending then descending volume as I approached the radio and turned it down and off. I got back to the phone and fumbled with the receiver as she screamed God-knows-what from the earpiece. Something about all this trouble over a blender.

"It's not a blender," I said again, or yelled.

"Then what the hell is it?" she said.

It's our little secret.

Good versus bad kept me quiet for a second, but I knew I had to say something to stall the inevitable barrage of abuse, or to prevent it if such a thing was possible, to keep the people who I was sure were listening, even if I couldn't be sure, from pitying me like I pitied so many of them. I had to say something powerful, something that cut like a knife.

"It's a knife," I said.

"A knife?" she said.

"An electric carving knife," I said.

She made a thinking sound, a hmm or a grunt. It wasn't dead air. She wasn't surprised. She was considering what I'd said, deciding whether or not to take it seriously. I was starting to think I might have turned the tide when she burst out laughing.

"A carving knife?" she said.

"An electric carving knife," I said.

"Well congratu-fucking-lations," she said before an arm came from over my shoulder and a finger depressed the button on the phone and the line went dead.

I followed my father's right arm from finger to shoulder and up into his eyes. They told me that bad had won. They told me to run, but I couldn't, because my father's other arm was around me and because I was frozen. He raised his right as though to swat me, and we heard Jane Grundy screaming from the receiver, saying either he or I didn't know who he or I was dealing with, that he or I was dead.

My father brought his whole hand down hard on the phone, grabbed it, yanking the cord from the jack, and threw the phone across the room. It slammed against the was leaning toward answering it too, if only to get out of my father's bedroom. I almost fell over when my father stood up.

He looked down at himself and brushed away the little bits of plaster that had settled on his pants with his palms. He nodded to me, went to the door and through it with a kind of dead-man-walking dignity. I waited a second before following slowly and at a certain distance.

I trailed him to the end of the hall, but stopped there, peeking my head around the corner and watching through the thin, black metal bars of the railing as he walked down the stairs, adjusted his shirt, brushed his pants again, and opened the door as the bell rang a third time.

There were two men on the other side of the door. The one in front was small and wiry, with short, dark hair and olive skin, and he was wearing a gray flannel suit with a skinny black tie. He had one arm behind his back, but I couldn't see anything in the reflection of the storm door because the guy behind him was holding it open with his back. He was tall and thick with a red face and wavy blond hair, and he wore nothing but a pair of sweatpants.

I'd seen enough gangster movies to know that the one in front, the little guy, was the brains, and the big guy was the muscle, which isn't to say that they were gangsters. They were from our neighborhood. I'd seen them both around, mowing lawns and getting home from work, though never together as far as I could remember.

wall. The bell tinkled. The phone dropped to the floor. The bell tinkled again.

My father watched it, followed it from his hand to the wall to the floor, and kept his eyes there once it had settled, still intact, on the carpet. His expression matched his question: "What have I done?"

Then another ringing, a different tone. I traced the sound back to its source—down the hall, taking a right before the kitchen, down half the stairs to the landing. The doorbell.

I didn't know whether I should answer it. We hadn't been expecting anyone, not in months, at least not anyone who bothered to ring the doorbell, and never at this time of night. I thought, maybe an old friend of the family who'd been driving home or around the neighborhood listening to Jane Grundy, maybe he or she'd had trouble sleeping or a fight with a husband or wife, had heard my father on the radio and decided to check in on us. Then again, it was possible Jane Grundy wasn't all bark. Maybe she'd sent a thug or two over to bite us for wasting her time.

My father had followed the phone cord to its end and was squatting down with it between his hands, examining the jack it had taken with it—along with a couple of chunks of plaster—from the wall.

"Forgive me," he said.

I didn't know if he was asking forgiveness from me or the phone. The doorbell rang again. It sounded a little more insistent, if that's possible. I was leaning toward thugs, but I

But being from our neighborhood didn't necessarily make them innocent—Jane Grundy was from our neighborhood too—and their timing was suspicious.

"I know it's late," said the brains.

He spoke fast, staccato, with a hint of an accent to match his green skin. My father stood facing him, had been facing him since opening the door. He'd seen the same movies I had and knew who was who. He didn't invite them in. He made no move to respond.

"We're sorry it's late," said the muscle, every syllable an effort.

"But we heard you got a carving knife," said the brains.

"An electric carving knife," muscle said.

My father looked over his shoulder and I pulled back around the corner behind the wall. It was odd to me how that simple movement, maybe a foot's difference, managed to muffle his voice.

It sounded like he said, "Where'd you hear that?"

I inched forward head-first until my eyes had made the corner. The muscle came into focus before the brains, maybe because there was so much more of him: the height, the width, the back of his head reflected in the storm door. I could see him waiting for the brains to speak for them, a struggle around his lips while the rest of his face rested blank, until he couldn't wait any longer.

"You were on the radio," he said.

The brains shot him a look like he'd spoken out of

turn, but he turned back to my father before the muscle could wrestle a response.

"It's all over the place," said brains. "The biggest thing to hit this neighborhood since slicing bread. Which you're fully equipped to do now that you got that knife, right?"

It sounded rhetorical even to me.

"Right?" said muscle.

Brains shot him another look. I couldn't tell if it was the atmosphere or the weather, but I felt hot, stuffy outside air fighting its way up the stairs to float around my face. Beyond the door, it was the kind of night where you could breathe the same breath for an hour if you stayed in the same spot waiting for a breeze. My forehead dampened. Brains turned back to my father.

"You don't have to answer that," said brains. "I wouldn't know if it worked on bread anyway."

"He doesn't have one," said muscle to my father.

"Neither do you," brains said, without a look back.

"So does it?" said muscle.

That one didn't sound rhetorical to me, but it must have sounded that way to my father because he just stood there, as though waiting for brains to take his turn. Brains seemed to have yielded the floor to my father, or tried to until he couldn't stand it any longer.

"Does it?" he said.

There was so much warmth around my head, it felt like it was melting, like the sweat was liquid face, the first symptom of a change of state. My father looked over his shoulder, more quickly this time. I'm not sure if he saw me or not before I ducked back behind the wall. It was cooler there. The corner formed some sort of boundary, keeping the hot air out and muffling my father's voice as he said, "Does it what?"

"Slice bread," muscle said.

Muscle's voice sounded the same, whether I was behind the wall or not. It had a woodwind timbre that went a long way toward making it clear he wasn't the brains of the operation. I peeked back out at him, at them.

"I don't know," my father said.

"It isn't like bread's the first thing you'd use it on," said brains, though it was unclear who he'd said it to.

"What is?" said muscle.

Muscle yielded to brains. Brains yielded to my father. My father looked over his shoulder, but I didn't duck behind the wall. He didn't see me anyway. He wasn't looking at anything, was probably just trying to figure out how to get rid of them. Brains couldn't stand it any longer.

"Meat, right?" he said. He was answering muscle and asking my father, "A nice roast beef or something?"

My father turned back to him, nodded distractedly, and lied: "Yes, beef."

"I bet it went right through like butter," said brains.

My father nodded. "Yes, butter, exactly."

"And then what?" said muscle.

I don't think my father knew what he meant. I didn't

know either. The heat was getting to me, and I was starting to feel some kind of tension in my shoulders. I didn't know if it was the fact that my father was lying—it was the first time my father had ever lied in front of me that I knew of, and I probably would have known he was lying even if I hadn't known he hadn't used it on a roast, something about the way he sighed the words, the same as the guy with the blender who turned out to be him—or the idea of the knife being used to cut beef, to cut anything at all.

My father made a stab at an answer: "I washed the blades, dried them, put everything back in the box."

"No," said brains. "He means what did you use it on next."

My father sighed one out without really trying. "I don't know," he said. "I don't remember."

"How could you not remember?" said brains. "How many times could you have used it?"

"I don't think he ever used it," said muscle.

Brains reached around and smacked muscle on the back of his head, almost before the line was out, as though to defend my father's honor. My father, who didn't want any violence on his account, on account of his lies, took a step back and raised his hands in a take-it-easy-guys kind of gesture that neither of them noticed, and he didn't say anything to call attention to himself. Muscle flinched and screwed up his face.

"I'm just saying," he said. "I don't even think he has one."

Maybe I was a naïve child, but I like to think I'd just been thrown off by the gangster scenario, the heat, the fasting. In any case, it didn't occur to me until that moment that we'd just been set up by a couple of bored, pathetic, bordering on middle-aged men who didn't have electric carving knives of their own to play with, that the brains didn't even look particularly brainy or the muscle particularly muscular, that I'd mostly just been rhyming their names, which were Mr. Danes and Mr. Russell, which I'd known for years having taken the school bus with their kids, having grown up in the same neighborhood, the same block.

It made me angry. It made my head ache. It made me want to lunge over the railing to pounce on them with the full force of twelve years' gravity, but it didn't stop me from salivating when Mr. Danes pulled a loaf of bread from behind his back and said, "Of course he does. Here's his chance to prove it."

I was hungry. For a moment, I didn't have to stomach the implications, the chance and the proof. I was focused on the bread.

My father showed a little more and a little less self-control. More in that the bread didn't seem to faze him. His eyes didn't follow the loaf as it swung from side to side like a hypnotist's watch, or if they did, the back of his head didn't show any sign of it. Like I said, I think he'd been sneaking food. Less because I didn't need to see his eyes to watch him deflate, and when he turned around,

beckoning Mr. Danes and Mr. Russell to follow with a
puppet-like flick of the wrist, he was fighting back tears,
eyes blinking, lips twitching.

They walked past without noticing or acknowledging
me and stopped just inside the kitchen.

Maria came in just behind them before the storm
door managed to close completely, but she didn't follow
them into the kitchen. She stopped in front of me, towering
over me in my slump against the wall.

"Hey," she said.

I wasn't trying to ignore her. It was just too much for
me. I was completely overwhelmed. It never even occurred
to me to say anything. I just turned my head away from her
and toward the men in the kitchen.

All I could see was Mr. Russell's huge bare back
filling the entryway, but I heard the crinkle of thin plastic,
Mr. Danes tearing the bread from its bag, and a soft-shoe
thunk as he set it on the counter.

I tried to picture his face as he did it. I wondered how
close he'd placed it to the knife. Closer, I was sure, than
any food had ever gotten, since I'd never seen food within
a few feet of it.

"I guess you're wondering what I'm doing here," said
Maria.

I had a sudden vision, a flash of inspiration—the
electric carving knife menaced by a three-course meal
in pencil on wide-ruled filler paper. The knife would be
cringing, but something, maybe in the quality of line or

the smooth, blocky shading, hinted that soon, in the next
panel, the food would be shredded to bits and placed on
platters to rot, in the final frame, unrecognizable in my
satisfied stomach.

I rushed back to my studio. Maria followed and I
didn't try to stop her. I just grabbed a pencil, and set to
without any of my usual preparations. No making sure
things were arranged neatly on my drafting table dresser,
no choosing the perfect, wrinkle-free sheet of paper, no
switching the radio to Jane Grundy. I didn't want order,
I didn't want clean paper, I didn't want to be soothed by
obscenity. I didn't know what I wanted, but for once I
didn't have to. Every attempt my mind made to ask me
was blocked by a humming in my head, steady, perfectly-
pitched, and loud enough to repel thought and allow action
without encouragement.

Lines scribbled themselves across the page, thick
and trunk-like, crushing the brittle thin ones with their
weight. Shadows cast in all directions, defying any
possible light source on or off the paper, though there
was a subtle glow to the knife, making it seem real—not
realistic, but lifelike, truthful, powerful, humming with
electricity, the same electricity humming in my ears.

Maria kept up a sparse but steady commentary,
from "It's like a studio in here," and "You got your own
supplies," to "You're really getting better," until I stopped.
I let my pencil fall to the paper. I listened. I looked down at
my drawing.

"What are you doing there?" said Maria.

It was terrible, even for a child: nothing but a series of dark streaks applied so forcefully that they'd torn through the sheet in places. There wasn't even a hint of a hum from the piece of paper. It was coming from down the hall.

"What are you doing here?" I said without looking up.

It was nothing but a rephrasing of what she'd said in the hallway a few minutes before, even if just now it was out of context, but it seemed to offend her, as though she was allowed to acknowledge that it was strange, her being there, or wrong, but not me.

"What do you mean?" she said.

"I thought it was time for us to move on," I said.

The hum held steady.

"It was," she said. "I mean," flustered, "that's not necessarily a bad thing," she said. "Moving on doesn't necessarily mean moving apart."

"Where's your dad?" I said.

She took so long to answer that I finally turned around.

"He's at our new place," she said.

But she said it quietly, like she was testing something.

"Why aren't you?" I said.

"Do you want to draw or something," she said. "Like we used to?"

I turned back to my desk and picked up the sheet of paper I'd just scarred with marks.

"This sucks," I said.

Her face kind of crinkled over as she looked at it, and her "I think it's pretty good," wasn't convincing.

"It's like you're developing your own style," she said, even less convincingly.

"You can have it then," I said, shoving it toward her.

She accepted it between thumb and forefinger and held it away from her like it was toxic, but she managed to keep her face admirably blank. I admit I enjoyed sitting there in silence watching the struggle, or I would have if we were actually sitting there in silence.

The humming seemed to be getting louder. I had to say something to cover it up, to smother it.

"When are you moving?" I said.

The question seemed to make her even more uncomfortable than the drawing.

"Soon," she said, and when she saw that that wasn't enough, "As soon as the place is ready I guess."

She might have gone on. She did go on. I saw her lips moving but I couldn't make anything of it out, couldn't hear it at all, because the humming kept getting louder until it was filling the house, overwhelming sound and taking over the space and frequencies that belong to the other senses. I saw the humming, felt it, smelled, tasted the hum until it seemed to be radiating, or failing to radiate, from my black hole of a head.

It was the knife.

My stomach realized it before I did, and before I realized there was nothing for my stomach to release, I was in the bathroom, huddled over the toilet, releasing nothing into it, but with a violence that made it feel like my eyeballs would pop—no—spill, out, because I was nothing but liquid by then. The hum began to co-opt other sounds, water drop echoes in the bathroom, the beat of the pulse in my temple, Maria's screaming. I retched for what must have been minutes, the hum of the knife reaching my ears from the kitchen, swelling counterpoint crescendos to my own shrieks and groans until I passed out, quivering like a beached jellyfish with my head against the bathtub.

I don't know how long I was under, but while I was, I dreamt that I was lying there when my father ran in, or up to me. I don't think we were in the bathroom, but I couldn't tell because it was black-dark. He was swinging the blood-dripping, almost blood-spraying, carving knife, and the hum began to buzz and then to roar.

I could see the blade shimmering like water in a cave, and his hand struggling to hang on to the knife, as though the knife were trying to get free of him, and the cord was trembling too, glinting sleek as far back in perspective as I could see.

As I tried to fight it or him off, not because I didn't deserve it—it wasn't a question of guilt or innocence—but because it seemed like what I was supposed to do, two little cherubim with the faces of Mr. Danes and Mr. Russell seesawed up and down on either side of him, chanting "congratu-fucking-lations" in harmony with the hum until it was replaced by a jarring silence, and then I came to: alone in the bathtub, fully clothed, the showerhead spraying me with cold water.

I sat up and looked over the edge, but I couldn't see much because the light was off or out and the door was closed. A thin sheet of light slid across the floor from beneath the door and glinted off what I thought was water, puddled shallow on the linoleum. My head dripped and plinked into the puddles.

I stood up slowly, aching with the effort of my dry-heaves and whatever had come after, and sloshed myself over the rim of the tub and onto the floor. I walked cautiously, waving my hands in front of me and side-to-side to stay clear of any obstacles. Water dripped in every direction. I planted my feet firmly with each separate step to keep from slipping, and my shoes squished audibly. It felt like my feet were sinking into the ground, my ankles into my feet.

I reached the door, pulled it open, and stepped out into the shadowy hallway. The lamp in the living room was bright enough to make me squint, and I stopped a moment to rub a sopping arm across my eyes.

My vision was still blurry, but I could make out a form at the end of the hallway, my father's, sitting slouched at the top of the stairs, and I moved toward it.

"Dad?" I said.

My father's figure resolved itself into my father. He was hunched over, cradling his hand. It was wrapped in a white towel streaked with red. He looked up then over at me. His eyes met mine, and mine were finally clear enough to see it. They were leaking all over his face. I looked down, embarrassed.

Down was a beige carpet, also streaked red. Blood running in various thicknesses of drizzle and drippings, at my feet, all the way back up the hallway behind me, and around again down toward my father before splitting left toward the kitchen.

I said, "Dad," again, and took another step closer. "Does it hurt?"

It was a strange question because I didn't know what I meant by it, but there was blood and tears and a hand wrapped in a bloody towel, and all of those things sounded and looked like pain to me, even if he didn't look like he was hurting.

I followed the trail of blood into the kitchen until it stopped dead at the cupboard to the left of the door. I didn't have to follow the lines of the cupboard up to the counter to know that it was the one the knife was resting on. It had been there since the day we'd finished cleaning up, the last time he'd touched it until Mr. Danes thunked the bread down beside it.

The bread was still there. The bulk of the loaf squatted heavy to the right of the knife. Three slices fanned out to the left. My father's left index finger lay crooked atop them, sliced clean through above the lowest knuckle. There was blood everywhere. I was dripping onto it, mixing with it, diluting it pink.

I grabbed the finger and stormed out of the kitchen to my father.

"What is this?" I said.

I shoved it up close to his face. I accused him with his own finger, of cutting it off, of letting them cut it off, of letting the knife cut it off, and he stared at it. He watched his finger accuse him and remained silent.

"How did this happen?" I said.

I stormed back into the kitchen, and grabbed the knife, but caught myself before ripping the cord from the wall like my father had the telephone. It was just a knife. It wasn't capable of cutting off a finger on its own.

I let my father's finger fall to the fan of bread and pulled the plug gently from the electrical outlet. I felt around for the tie, found it, coiled the cord and twisted it. I grabbed a paper towel, dampened it against my shirt, and swabbed the blood from the knife and blades.

I took the knife in one hand and the finger in the other and went back out to ask my father one last time: "How did it happen?" and when he didn't answer, I left home to find out on my own.

I'd forgotten about the weather. The air was hot and thick and stagnant despite the hour, and rather than cool me, the water that was still soaking me warmed seasonably and I began to sweat almost immediately. I slashed the space in front of me with the knife and moved into the vacuum it created, toward Mr. Danes' house, two doors up.

I could see a light on in the second floor window and a silhouette against the light, and because every house in our neighborhood was identical, not counting shades of vinyl siding and shutters, wallpaper and carpet, I knew that Mr. Danes was in his living room. I reached for the bell, but decided to knock, to keep from waking his wife and kids.

I knocked and stepped backward away from the door to get a better view of what happened in the window. The silhouette slipped away, and suddenly the light went out. I counted ten-one-thousand, but still the door didn't open. Another ten and I knocked again.

I tried the handle, but the door was locked so I went around to the hedges. I shoved my father's finger into my front pocket to free up a hand, and used the hand to dig around in the dirt for a pebble, something to lob at Mr. Danes' living room window, like in the movies.

All I could find was a rock the size of my fist. I tried to lob it lightly, but it didn't make it three feet above my head before turning around and heading back down. I threw it again, hoping to add another ten feet to its upward trajectory, and I did, but its downward trajectory took it through Mr. Danes' living room window and onto his carpet followed by jagged glass.

The light came back on and the silhouette reappeared. It came all the way up to the window and inspected the scraps of glass still jutting from the frame. I wished I could have been up there to shove its head all the way through, to shove it from side to side into them, but he didn't even slide it through on its own. He stopped on his side of the window as though the glass was still separating us. His "You broke my window," proved that he was aware it wasn't.

"Why'd you break my window?" he said.

"You wouldn't open the door," I said.

"It's gonna be expensive to replace," he said.

I reached into my pocket and pulled out my father's finger.

"So is this," I said.

It didn't exactly make sense. I didn't know if they made prosthetic fingers, and if they did, we were fully insured, but I thought I'd made my point.

"What is it?" he said.

Even in the darkness outside, his face silhouetted by the light within, I could seem him squinting, jutting his head forward and inch or so and then pulling back two, reminded by a glint from the edge of a shard of the invisible boundary that kept us separate.

"Why don't you come down and see," I said.

The silhouette hesitated before disappearing from the window. I took a few steps closer but didn't open the storm door. I just held the finger up to it so it would be the first thing he saw when he opened the front door from the other side.

I should have known the first thing he'd see would be his own reflection. He turned the landing light on as he made his way down the stairs, and because it was dark on my side, he had to squint again to make out anything beyond the glass.

The first thing I saw was a hand held to a stomach, wrapped in a towel streaked with blood. He was still squinting when I let my own hand, the one holding my father's finger, drop to my side.

"What is it?" said Mr. Danes.

His voice was muffled by the door. I moved closer, to make sure that I was right about his hand. I got so close that my breath fogged the glass, and when I wiped my breath away with my arm, the water on my sleeve smeared and warped the image. Even as the drops dripped to the bottom of the pane, I could see that he was another casualty. Of the knife, of Mr. Russell, I couldn't decide.

"You, too," I said.

I knew that my voice would be just as muffled as his,

but I'd expected him to be able to hear me at that range, so when he said, "What?" I raised the knife.

He shrugged and said, "What?" again.

I was off, at a run this time, toward Mr. Russell's house, across the street and another block up, with the knife held out in front of me like a sword. The sweat stung my eyes and dropped salty on my tongue. I approached panting and out of breath, shoving my father's finger back into my pocket.

From the curb, I could see a dark shape on the front stoop and a small, orange spark, now bright, now dim, floating the points of a triangle—Mr. Russell, seated, slouching, smoking a cigarette. As I moved toward him, his knees distinguished themselves, level with the bare shoulders in the shadows behind them, and the elbows propped on the knees made his forearms a table for his chin.

He'd noticed me by then. The only sign of it was the way the cigarette stopped brightening, stopped moving, stayed smoldering at his elbow. He didn't look up until I was just a couple of feet away, towering over him with the knife in my hand. Even then he didn't look like he cared much why, not that I could see very clearly in the darkness with my sweat-stung eyes.

"What can I do for you?" he said.

His voice sounded windy, but it didn't sound stupid. It sounded tired, so tired it reminded me how tired I was and let me feel it too. I was still breathing heavily. I noticed it, along with the pulse in my ears, as the exhaustion crept over me. Water dripped from my clothes, as though reluctantly, onto his front walk.

Mr. Russell remembered his cigarette, took one last drag from it, and stubbed it at his feet. He patted the space beside him on the stoop, motioning for me to join him. I didn't even think about it. I slunk toward it and slumped down, maybe a little harder than was good for me.

He gave me a moment to catch my breath, to collect myself, and asked me again: "What can I do for you?"

I raised the knife half-heartedly and without looking at him.

"Why'd you do it?" I said.

"Can I see it?" he said.

He reached for the knife before I had a chance to respond. I didn't give it to him, but I let it go without a struggle. I could see him examining it out of the corner of my eye. He turned it over in his hands, flicked the orange switch on, off, brought it to his eye like the scope of a gun.

"Your father wouldn't let me touch it," he said.

He wiped the blade on the calf of his sweats and lowered it to his left index finger, miming or imagining. I scooted over a little and turned my head to watch him directly. He pressed the blade harder into his flesh. I could tell by the way the skin on either side of it formed a valley. When he pulled it away, it left little teeth marks, though the knife hadn't quite broken the skin.

"Did you do it on purpose?" I said.

He turned his head, squinting at me, as though trying to make me out at a distance, slouching further and looking slightly upward to account for perspective. It was like he was trying to decide whether the person coming toward him was friend or foe, but I wasn't moving at all.

There was the water, drip-dripping to the stoop.

"I went over to Mr. Danes' house afterward," he said. "He was jealous, even afterwards."

"But you don't have one either," I said.

He laughed to himself, and wagged the knife, tapping the tip of the blade against his head. I didn't know if he meant I was right, that that had been absent-minded of him, or that possession was nine-tenths of the law. I tensed and he laughed again.

"He thought he could make one with a steak knife and a cake mixer," he said.

"So you didn't do it yourself?" I said.

He showed me his hands—ten fingers, the five on the left curled lightly around the electric carving knife, the five on the right spread-wide, veins showing just beneath the surface of the tanned skin on the back of his hand, making him look strong and vulnerable to sharp objects at the same time. I wondered which one he'd used on my father.

"I mean you didn't cut Mr. Danes' finger off yourself," I said.

I had to stand up to pull my father's finger from my pocket. Mr. Russell startled and the carving knife dropped from his hand to the stoop with a clatter. I snatched it up as casually as I could but didn't give it back to him. His eyes widened as though I'd finally reached him.

"Why the fuck would I do that?" he said.

"Why the fuck did you do it to my father?" I said.

I clenched my teeth and gripped the knife more tightly. He'd left his hands out in front of him, resting the fish-belly underside of his forearms against his knees, assuming the position. I wanted to put blade to wrist—a hand, an arm, a neck for a finger, one after the next. It was the battle of good against bad again. I couldn't even lift my arm.

"Who?" he said.

"My father," I said.

"No," he said. "Who distracted him?" he said. "Who made the knife slip when he started screaming, puking like a little baby?"

"It wasn't me screaming," I said. "It was Maria."

A breeze started to blow. I saw it first, the pale hairs on the back of Mr. Russell's hand trembling, then I felt it cool against my wet skin, trying to dry it taught. The air thinned and I breathed it deeply, getting a little high. I let it go like a nervous cough and feeling returned to my arm.

"Well it sounded like a girl," he said. "But when we got to the bathroom all we found was you, wrapped around the toilet in a puddle of your own puke."

I wondered how Maria could have gotten by them unnoticed, but that wasn't the most important thing just then. The most important thing was who was to blame. Maybe I had distracted my father. Maybe he'd even cut his own finger off because of it. But I'd spent the last week trying, in my own way, to bring him to his senses.

"I wasn't the one who tricked him into using it in the

first place," I said.

Before he could answer I brought the knife up over my head and down hard. I think I'd been aiming for his wrist, but his shoulder got in the way. The serrated blade scraped off a layer of skin around the socket. He didn't wince. He didn't even flinch. I felt dizzy.

"We even?" he said.

I didn't say anything, but whatever I did—breathed in, breathed out—must have looked like an affirmation, because he said, "Then go settle up with your father."

I got up and walked off with every intention of doing it, sooner or later. The breeze got stronger, turned into a wind, and the first drops of rain speckled the street around my feet. I couldn't see them in the dark, or feel it, but I could hear them landing with a smack, in ones and twos, then countless. I was heading down the street in the direction of my house as it started to pour as if someone had severed the sky. I was freshly soaked by the time I got to Mrs. Malatendi's door.

I expected to have to wait even longer for an answer there than at Mr. Danes'. I knew Maria wouldn't answer, not that late at night, not after what had happened. And I could only guess how long it would take Mrs. Malatendi to wake up to the sound of the doorbell, get out of bed, walk up or down the stairs (depending on where her room was) to the landing, and get the door open.

No matter how long you gave me, I never would have guessed right, because right turned out to be immediate. I rang, she answered, standing in the doorway, fully clothed, as though she'd been expecting me. More unnerving—she didn't even seem displeased. I took the time I'd expected to spend waiting to collect myself, then opened the storm door, having finally learned my lesson.

"Mrs. Malatendi?" I said.

It came out sounding like I wasn't sure it was her. I was but I wasn't. She was but she wasn't.

"It's kind of late for you to be out, isn't it?" she said, in confirmation, I think, or denial.

"Can I talk to Maria for a minute?" I said.

Mrs. Malatendi looked scared for a minute, but then returned to abnormal.

"She didn't tell you, honey?" she said. "She's gone to

live with her father."

"But she was just…"

I didn't finish. I just kind of pointed over my shoulder toward my house. I knew I wasn't crazy. I knew she'd been there with me as I scribbled my mess, as I passed out. But I knew there was no point in arguing.

I hoped I'd have better luck back home.

From the landing, everything looked pretty much as I'd
left it. The light was on in the kitchen, but the rest of the
house was dark. There might have been a few more blood
stains on the stairs, because my father was gone. Asleep
on the couch, I assumed.

I searched the rest of the house for Maria, sure she
wouldn't be downstairs with my father, that there was no
point in that. But she wasn't in the studio, my bedroom,
the bathroom, the living room.

I made my way up to the kitchen and turned left,
looking down at the counter, the blood, the bread in its
place. I set the knife down between the slices and the loaf
and plugged the cord into the electrical outlet. I noticed
the finger still in my hand, placed it crooked atop the fan
of slices, and left my left hand beside it, eyeing the knife,
my hand, the finger, one at a time and all in together.

I reached for the knife with my right but didn't quite
touch it before letting it dangle back to my side. I looked
around the room in which I'd spent the better part of my
time during the past week and could barely remember why,
and if I could barely remember, I could hardly understand.

I reached for the knife again, gripped it as firmly as
I could given how wet I was, and brought the blade to my

index finger, pressing it into the flesh like Mr. Russell had.

I pulled the knife back some and flicked the orange switch. The knife hummed to an imitation of life, vibrating in my hand, sending a tickle up my arm and across my shoulders. I slashed at the air in front of me with it. I slashed at the loaf of bread.

I turned off the knife, set it back in its place, and grabbed some of the bread, shoving it into my mouth by the fistful. The act of chewing felt foreign to my mouth. It couldn't salivate fast enough to put the bread down, and I breathed rapidly and loudly through my nose to keep from choking. I could feel each bit I swallowed wind its way down my throat and land heavily in my stomach, sending it back to work with an ache.

I looked back at the knife, but the sound of the rain against the roof, the windows and the wind in the trees distracted me, made me forget again what I meant to do with it. I went over and switched on the radio, but Jane Grundy had finally succeeded in putting her audience to sleep, leaving static in the neighborhood's wake like a simulcast of the rain outside.

I left it on and went back to the tableau, awaiting inspiration I don't know how long, trying to find my place in it. The rain didn't let up, but the static did. It gave in to a click and some feedback and a voice that sounded a lot less expressive than I remembered, though it was undoubtedly her.

"Couldn't sleep," she said. "Couldn't stop thinking

about that caller."

I didn't know if she meant me or my father or somebody who'd called later.

"The kid with the knife," she said. "Kid: if you're listening, you know what to do."

But I didn't. I didn't know if she meant for me to call her, or use the knife on somebody or something, or just shut her off and out of my hearing until the next time I was having trouble sleeping.

"That finger's gonna go bad," she said.

I didn't know how she knew about the finger, but it didn't surprise me either, and I didn't stop to consider the ways she might. I got stuck on the biology of it. There was no point in putting the finger on ice; it was probably too late to reattach it anyway, and I had no intention of finding and waking my father.

I ran back to my studio, following the trail of blood as far as the master bathroom, grabbed a jar of shellac, and brought it back to the kitchen. I hadn't used it in a while, and it was a struggle to open, but I finally got the lid off, pouring it over my father's finger and its bed of bread.

"It's no use," said Jane Grundy. "Maybe counting sheep."

She began counting, from one, steady but not rhythmic. I swirled the shellac to the speed of sheep, jumping over the fence, or whatever it was she was imagining them doing, watching the glaze ooze from the lip of the jar, pooling on the surface of the finger and the bread and spreading out in slow waves.

There must have only been ten sheep, because she started going backwards from there. I imagined them: the same ten, forced to jump over the fence or through hoops, or just to walk through the gate to the pen all night long for the sake of our sleep. I thought how unfair it was that one got a break, while ten had to go back right away, though eventually things would work out for most of them. I thought about things working out.

As she got back to four, I realized that the jar was empty. I had no idea how long it had been but I set it down on the counter. I picked up the knife and gripped it hard, trying to pinpoint the place where knives ended and fingers began, the place where flesh separates from flesh to reveal our true essence, our responsibility: to ourselves, to each other, living and dead. I imagined sheep one panting, exhausted, from running back and forth to give us a rest, a break, knowing that it was only three, now two, from going again, while sheep ten relaxed, maybe even napped, on the other side of the gate or pen. I wondered if they took turns from one night to the next, if they had a sense of fairness, of compassion for each other, or if they were more cutthroat about it, but realized I would never know either way. They all looked the same to me.

I flipped on the switch and began with one.